Simon's Escape

A Story of the Holocaust

Bonnie Pryor

Enslow Publishers, Inc.
40 Industrial Road
Box 398
Berkeley Heights, NJ 07922
USA

http://www.enslow.com

Library of Congress Cataloging-in-Publication Data:

Pryor, Bonnie.

Simon's escape : a story of the Holocaust / Bonnie Pryor.

p. cm. — (Historical fiction adventures (HFA))

Summary: Simon, a young Polish Jew, and his family are forced by Nazis to leave their home for the filth and hunger of the Warsaw ghetto then, when his family is all taken away, he escapes to fight for survival in the countryside.

ISBN 978-0-7660-3388-7 (Library Ed.)

ISBN 978-1-59845-216-7 (Paperback Ed.)

1. Holocaust, Jewish (1939-1945)—Poland—Juvenile fiction. 2. Jews—Poland—Juvenile fiction. 3. World War, 1939-1945—United States—Juvenile fiction. 4. Poland—History—1918-1945—Juvenile fiction. [1. Holocaust, Jewish (1939-1945)—Poland. 2. Jews—Poland—Fiction. 3. World War, 1939-1945—United States—Fiction. 4. Family life—Poland—Fiction. 5. Poland—History—1918-1945—Fiction.] I. Title.

PZ7.P94965Sim 2010

[Fic]—dc22   2009029322

Printed in the United States of America

062010 Lake Book Manufacturing, Inc., Melrose Park, IL

10 9 8 7 6 5 4 3 2 1

To Our Readers:

We have done our best to make sure all Internet Addresses in this book were active and appropriate when we went to press. However, the author and the publisher have no control over and assume no liability for the material available on those Internet sites or on other Web sites they may link to. Any comments or suggestions can be sent by e-mail to comments@enslow.com or to the address on the back cover.

✪ Enslow Publishers, Inc., is committed to printing our books on recycled paper. The paper in every book contains 10% to 30% post-consumer waste (PCW). The cover board on the outside of each book contains 100% PCW. Our goal is to do our part to help young people and the environment too!

Illustration Credits: Enslow Publishers, Inc., p. 155; Original Painting by © Corey Wolfe, p. 1; United States Holocaust Memorial Museum (USHMM), p. 158; USHMM, courtesy of Joanne Schartow, p. 156.

Cover Illustration: Original Painting by © Corey Wolfe.

Contents

chapter one

War!

September 1939, Warsaw, Poland

When the first bomb fell, Simon and his friend Adam were jumping on the bed in Simon's room. It was forbidden, of course, but the boys were bored after being cooped up in school on such a beautiful day. The boys looked alike enough to be mistaken for brothers. Both were short and sturdy with sandy blond hair and blue eyes—although Adam was Polish and Simon's family was Jewish. They were supposed to be doing homework together, but the boys had started wrestling. Simon's mother was out at one of her charity events, and his father was at work in his office that connected to the back of the apartment. Lydia, the Polish cook, was busy downstairs in the kitchen.

"What was that?" Simon asked, freeing himself from Adam's stranglehold and sitting up. They heard it again. Boom! Simon ran to his bedroom window. He looked out in time to see a German plane flying so low over the luxurious apartment building he lived in that the windows rattled. The apartment was two stories, with four large bedrooms on the upper floor. Simon's room was at the end of a long hallway. The boys clattered down the graceful, curved staircase, just as Simon's brother, Jozef, burst through the door. His face was pale. "The Germans are attacking. They are shooting people in the streets."

It was not unexpected, although now that it was actually happening, it was a shock. For weeks, rumors of an attack had been circulating. At school, the music teacher had devoted the entire period to singing patriotic songs. Many people had made arrangements to leave the city, but Simon's father had been reluctant to close his factory that made fur coats and hats.

"I'd better get home," Adam said before Simon could stop him. He ducked out the door to the streets. The wide street in front of Simon's apartment was lined with shade trees. It was usually quiet, but now it was clogged with horses, wagons, and cars. Simon watched his friend weave his way through the crowds of frightened people until he disappeared around the corner. Simon's father, Mr. Gorski, ran through the door to his office just as Lydia ran in from the kitchen, carrying Anya, Simon's little sister. Mr. Gorski took his daughter in his arms.

"Go to the cellar under the factory," he told Lydia. "I think we will be safe there."

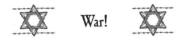

Another plane flew over and Simon heard the rapid fire of machine guns. Out in the crowded streets, the people were screaming.

"They are shooting civilians," Lydia cried out.

"Quickly!" Mr. Gorski shouted. Fortunately, they did not have to go out into the streets because the back door led directly to Mr. Gorski's office. Beyond that was a small warehouse, where employees sewed fur coats. Just as they left, the phone rang. Motioning them ahead, Mr. Gorski grabbed the receiver.

They hurried through the office and into the factory, then down a narrow set of stairs to a small room, lit only with a bare bulb hanging from the ceiling. The room had a dirt floor with several trunks for places to sit. Seven of Simon's father's employees were there already, along with Mr. Stanick, the factory manager. Mr. Gorski joined them a few seconds later. "That was your mother," he said. "She is safe and will come home as soon as she can."

Anya's eyes filled with tears. "I don't like this place, Daddy," she said. "And I forgot my dolly."

"I got it for you," Lydia said soothingly, as she retrieved the doll from the oversized pockets of her apron. She pulled Anya onto her lap and softly sang Polish children's songs to her. Anya was only four, and although Lydia loved Simon and Jozef, everyone knew Anya was her favorite.

Simon wished his father would put his arm around him and tell him they would be all right. But he was nearly ten years old, and he knew his father expected him to act brave, even if he didn't feel that way. He looked at his brother sitting stiff and pale beside him. Jozef was thin and dark haired. He wore glasses because of his weak eyes. Jozef was twelve and the top student in his class at school. He was already two grades ahead of other boys his age. He planned on going to the university to become a doctor. All of Simon's teachers expected him to be clever like Jozef, but Simon had more interest in playing soccer than studying.

"What is going to happen now?" Jozef asked.

Their father shook his head. "Adolf Hitler, the leader of the Nazi Party in Germany, seems to have plans to conquer all of Europe. The Nazis believe that the Germans are the 'master race,' and they want to conquer more territory for Germany."

"Do you think we can beat them?" Simon asked.

Mr. Gorski shook his head. "I don't know. Poland does not have much of an army and the Germans have been building theirs for years."

Mr. Stanick spoke up. "We had better hope our army wins. I have heard some of Hitler's speeches on the radio. He is scornful of the Polish people and he hates the Jews."

After several hours, there were no more sounds of bombs or planes. Simon's father went upstairs to see if it was safe.

Simon waited fearfully. He thought about playing soldiers with the other boys at school, and how they had talked about war and how exciting it would be. This was not exciting. It was terrifying.

Except for a broken window, the apartment had not been damaged. The streets outside, however, were in chaos. From his bedroom window, Simon could see bodies lying in the street, with pools of blood surrounding them. A horse had fallen in the street, thrashing in agony, still attached to a wagon. He saw a man crying as he knelt next to the bodies of a woman and a small child. Simon had never seen a dead person before, and his stomach churned in fear. What kind of people would shoot at a woman and child? He watched anxiously for his mother, sighing with relief when he saw her making her way through the crowded street. He flew down the street to meet her and threw his arms around her.

"They were shooting people right on the street," he cried. "A woman was killed, right in front of our house. And a horse."

"You poor thing," Simon's mother said. "Were you terribly frightened?"

"Not too much," Simon said, trying to sound braver than he felt.

That night, Simon's mother and father talked late into the evening. Simon crept out of his room and sat by his parent's room, eavesdropping.

"We should leave," he heard his mother say.

"Where would we go? How would I make a living?" Simon's father answered. In the end, Simon's father decided that they would be safer staying where they were. At first, it seemed that he was right. The raids continued for a week, but none of them damaged the apartment, although several times Simon's family had to take refuge in the cellar. Jozef and his father listened to the radio, but no one really knew what was happening. The Polish army seemed to be on the run, but there had not been a formal surrender.

A few nights later, after Lydia had cleared the plates from the large mahogany table in the dining room, Mr. Gorski asked Simon and Jozef to stay seated. His face looked grim.

"You boys are old enough to know what is going on," he said. "As you know, Hitler and his Nazi Party have complete control of Germany. Hitler hates the Jews. He says we are a subhuman, evil race who want to take over the world. A few years ago, the Nazis took every book written by a Jew out of the libraries in Germany and burned them. He is obsessed with a pure German race and doesn't want anything Jewish to contaminate the 'master race.' Unfortunately, he has many supporters who are all too happy to follow him. Last November, in Germany and its surrounding territories, the SS—the chief security force of the Nazis—went everywhere, breaking into Jewish-owned

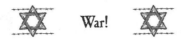

businesses and homes, destroying property. They burned down synagogues. About a hundred people were killed, and thousands were rounded up and sent to concentration camps. So many windows were broken, they called it *Kristallnacht,* the night of broken glass. The Nazis claim that the Jews in Germany provoked the attack, but those claims are not true. I am sure the Nazis will make life miserable for us, but what can they do when there are so many of us? Warsaw has over a million people, and at least a third of them are Jews."

*****

Less than a week later, the Germans roared into town with tanks, three-wheeled motorcycles, and smartly stepping soldiers. Simon and Jozef watched from their window.

Mr. Gorski told them sharply, "Stay away from the windows."

Simon sat on a chair. "Everyone else is out in the streets, watching."

"The Poles. You won't see any Jews out there. I got through to your Aunt Ester in Lodz this morning on the phone. She said the Poles are going into the houses of Jews who fled the city and they're stealing everything."

"We have lots of Polish friends," Simon said.

"I think we will soon find out if they really are friends," Mr. Gorski said.

"Just last week one of my teachers was telling the class about the 'dirty Jews.' She said we killed their Christ, and we were all rich because we cheated everyone else. She also said we were communists," Jozef said. "I was sitting right there. Everyone just looked at me."

"Why didn't you tell me?" Mr. Gorski asked.

Jozef shrugged. "She has said things before. Most of my teachers are not like that."

"Maybe we should leave," Simon's mother said fearfully.

"Where would we go? The radio said hundreds were killed trying to cross the river into Russia. Some made it, but not many," Mr. Gorski said.

For a few days nothing happened. When the radio announced that the schools—closed for several weeks during the fighting—were reopening, Simon was relieved. It was boring sitting at home all day and he missed his friends. When he reached the school, however, the headmaster met him at the door. "Go home," he said, not allowing Simon to enter the building.

Simon was bewildered, as he saw other children enter the school. "The radio said the schools were reopening today," he said.

"Not for Jews," the headmaster said harshly. "Go to your own school."

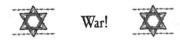

Several older boys heard the headmaster's remarks. "My parents say you dirty Jews are going to get what's coming to you," they said, laughing. They threw stones at Simon while the headmaster stood and watched.

Simon ran home, trying to keep from crying. Jozef was already home. "You too?" he asked.

Simon stomped his foot. "It's not fair! How can they do that to us?"

Mr. Gorski had even worse news. "The Nazis say that no Jew can own a business, except for a few grocery stores and bakeries that only sell to Jews. I had to sign the business over to Mr. Stanick, my manager."

Simon's mother looked worried. "Can we trust him?"

"Stanick has worked for me for ten years. I trust him as well as anyone. He promises to give me a share of the profits. I have a paper saying that when the war is over, he will return ownership to me. What else could I do? The banks have frozen our accounts, too. They will only allow us to withdraw two hundred fifty zloty a week."

Mrs. Gorski looked pale. "How will we live?"

"The Germans have set up a Jewish council. A man named Adam Czerniaków will be at the head," Mr. Gorski answered. "They will start up committees to help solve these problems."

The next morning, Lydia came to say she could no longer work for them. "My husband thinks it is too dangerous," she said, with tears running down her face. "He has never been happy that I was working for Jews."

"We would have had to let you go anyway," Mrs. Gorski said gently. "The Nazis have left us just barely enough money to buy food."

Simon was stunned. Lydia had been part of the family for as long as he could remember. She always had a sweet snack for them when he and Jozef came home from school, and it was Lydia whom he often talked to when his busy parents were not home. He stood stiffly when she hugged him good-bye, trying not to cry. "Be brave," she whispered.

Simon watched her board the trolley. Be brave? How could he be brave? It was all he could do to stand all the changes the Germans had made in his life. Jews were no longer allowed to use the libraries. They could only ride certain trolleys. His parents would hardly let him step out the door. They feared for his safety. He sat in the house all day, bored and irritable.

The Jewish council was required to issue and enforce the Nazi orders. The men on the council were appointed by Nazi leaders and were not given a choice whether they would serve or not. As soon as they were in place, the SS started issuing decrees. One of the first laws the council issued was that every Jewish male from ages sixteen to sixty had to register for work. Shortly after that they announced that all Jews older than the age of ten had to wear a white

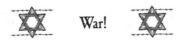

armband with a blue star whenever they went out. Almost overnight the streets were full of vendors hawking the armbands. Mrs. Gorski bought a stack and spent all day dutifully sewing them onto the family's shirts and coats.

Simon hated the armband. People on the street stared at him with unfriendly faces when he walked by. The Polish children mocked him. Mrs. Gorski sewed the hated symbol on all his clothes because anyone not obeying the new law could be shot.

Mr. Gorski registered for work. The Germans used the forced labor to clean up the rubble from the bombing and to shovel snow off the streets. The work was backbreaking. Mr. Gorski received ration cards for his labor. The ration cards only allowed a small amount of food, not even enough to keep a person alive. Polish farmers brought in food to sell to the few Jewish stores that had been allowed to stay open. But they took advantage of their Jewish neighbors with high prices.

At first, Simon's family managed to live fairly well. Mr. Stanick brought money from the factory, and Mr. Gorski was able to purchase enough food to supplement the meager rations. Simon's mother, who had never learned how to cook, gamely tried to make nourishing meals. Luckily, the phones still worked, and Mrs. Gorski was able to get instructions from Lydia until she was able to fix simple soups and stews. She also learned how to make noodles from the flour rations. One morning she even made Simon's favorite breakfast treat—*flampletzle*, a little round, flat, baked dough, spread with butter and cream.

"This is just as good as Lydia's," Simon told his mother.

"Even better," Jozef declared.

The winter of 1939 into 1940 was unusually cold. The house was heated by burning coal. To make the coal last as long as possible and to save money, Simon's family closed off the four bedrooms and only heated the kitchen and living room. One day, after Mr. Gorski returned from work, he sat by the small stove, trying to warm his hands. He slumped in his chair.

"What has happened?" Simon's mother asked.

"A man fell to the ground, weak with hunger and cold. The SS officer in charge of the work group told him to get up. But he was just too weak. So the officer shot him. Then, on the way home, an old man was walking down the street with a small bag of groceries. Some Poles began taunting him and they knocked the sack out of his hands. Then they put a big sign around his neck that said '*Jude*' (Jew) and threw rocks and rotten food at him. Some SS men were watching and laughing and encouraging the Poles," Mr. Gorski said sadly, looking at his wife. "I did nothing to help him. I just hurried away, glad that they had not noticed me."

16

"They would have turned on you," Mrs. Gorski said. "There was nothing you could do."

Suddenly, there was a rough knock at the door and a German voice shouted.

"Open up!"

Four soldiers pushed their way past Mr. Gorski when he opened the door. The soldiers pulled open drawers and tipped over tables, searching the house. "Do you have guns or radios?" one of them barked.

Mr. Gorski pointed to the radio. "Only that," he said. One of the soldiers scooped it up. "Jews are forbidden to have radios," he said. On his way out the door, one of them ripped the telephone from the wall and took that, too.

Simon had stood frozen while the soldiers ransacked the house. When they left he watched his gentle brother Jozef hit his fist into his other hand. "I wish we had a gun," he said bitterly. "I would have killed them all."

chapter two

The Ghetto

1940

Somehow Simon's family made it through the cold winter and the summer that followed, although every day there were new restrictions for Jews. For a while, Simon attended the Jewish school, but he was not comfortable there. Everyone in the school spoke Yiddish—a language spoken mainly by Eastern European Jews. But Simon had never learned it.

Many of the Jews in Warsaw stayed in their own neighborhoods, speaking Yiddish. They did not bother to learn to speak Polish well, even though some families had been there for generations. But Simon's parents considered themselves Poles, and most of their friends were Polish. They were not religious and seldom observed the Jewish rituals, nor had they taught the boys Yiddish. This meant that Simon was forced to sit with the younger children at school while he learned the new language.

One day, Simon stopped at a park on his way home from school. Some of his old non-Jewish friends were there, playing soccer. Simon was a good soccer player, and before the war he was always picked first when teams were made.

"This park is not for dirty Jews," one boy shouted. "Get out of here."

Simon's friend Adam was there. "We're not allowed to play with you," he said. "This park is only for Polish kids."

"I am Polish," Simon objected. "I was born right here, same as you."

"You are not the same as us," another boy shouted. "You're a dirty Jew." The other boys picked up the chant: "Dirty Jew. Dirty Jew."

Simon saw that Adam did not take part in the taunting, but neither did he object. He turned and ran home, their laughter ringing in his ears.

*****

In October 1940, the Germans ordered all Jews to move into the crowded, rundown section in the center of Warsaw. Mr. Gorski rented a wagon to carry some of their belongings. Simon looked around fearfully. Among the apartment buildings were dilapidated factories and warehouses. There were no parks or even patches of grass or trees anywhere. The streets were congested with desperate-looking people. Simon's family stood in line for hours along with other families displaced by the German decree. At last, a Jewish council member handed them a paper with their new address. It was on the second floor of a big building and it was only a small kitchen, a living room, and a tiny bathroom.

"I hate this place," Simon cried out. "It's dirty and it smells. I want to go home."

"This is our home now," Jozef said bitterly.

Simon's mother stood inside the doorway, surveying their tiny new home. Then she straightened her shoulders. "This will be cozy," she said, trying to sound cheerful.

Simon saw a bug scurry behind the rusty kitchen sink and he shivered. He wiped tears from his eyes with his fists. His mother hugged him. "This won't last forever," she said soothingly.

Mr. Gorski had planned on making several trips to bring their belongings, but the apartment was so small that he realized they would have to leave most of their things behind. Simon and Jozef helped unload the wagon. The streets were clogged with other people doing the same thing.

"I have to take the wagon back," Mr. Gorski said.

"Can I come with you?" Simon asked, anxious to escape the apartment.

Mr. Gorski nodded. "We will have to walk back. Your mother gave me a list of small items we forgot. You can help me carry them."

When they arrived at their old apartment, Mr. Gorski reached for his key. To their surprise, Mr. Stanick opened the door. He looked embarrassed.

"The Germans told me to move here so I would be close to the factory," he said. He did not look directly at Simon's father while he spoke. "There is more bad news, I am afraid. The Germans have confiscated all the furs. The factory is now going to make uniforms and coats for the German army. There will be a German overseer, so I will no longer be able to send you money."

Mr. Gorski did not answer him. He went about the apartment gathering the items on the list. At the door he turned back. "You go to church every Sunday. Is this what your church says is the Christian thing to do?"

Mr. Stanick lost his embarrassed look, and his face reddened with anger. "You should have left when you had the chance. This country will be better off when all you Jews are gone," he said, sneering.

Simon was stunned. Mr. Stanick had always been friendly and nice to him. His family had been to their house for dinner on many festive occasions. He had played soccer with Mr. Stanick's sons and considered them friends.

"The Germans didn't assign you this apartment," Mr. Gorski said. "You just took it—and the business."

"For years I was humiliated working for a Jew," Mr. Stanick said through clenched teeth. "Now it is my time.

The Germans know how to keep you Jews in place. Go live with the rest of your kind!" He slammed the door, the look of hate on his face unmistakable.

Simon's father seemed to age instantly. His shoulders slumped and he walked slowly as though he were carrying a heavy burden. Simon looked at his father. He had always been a handsome man, with dark hair and a full mustache. For the first time, Simon noticed the dark circles under his father's eyes and his sagging skin. After a while Mr. Gorski spoke.

"He's right. We should have gone to Palestine or even America. I was afraid that if I did, the Germans would take my factory."

"Maybe when the Germans leave, you can get it back," Simon said.

Mr. Gorski nodded. "Perhaps you are right. At least things can't get much worse. The clerk in the housing office said that there are more than 350,000 people squeezed into a little more than 2 percent of the city."

*****

Simon gradually adjusted to the new "Jewish Quarter," or ghetto, and even managed to make a friend—a boy named Abram, who lived a few blocks away. He got used to the smell of unwashed bodies and clogged sewers. The council tried to keep up with the needs of the people. With money

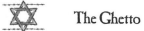

sent from America, they set up soup kitchens and started up several schools. There was even some entertainment, like concerts and plays. But more and more people were forced to live in the quarter. Jews arrived from small towns, many with little more than the clothes on their backs, and it was impossible to keep up.

"I heard there are more than 400,000 people here now," Jozef told Simon. "And more are coming every day."

At first, there was a lot of traffic in and out of the ghetto. Mr. Gorski was able to trade valuables he had brought with them for needed food. One day Lydia came for a visit. She lived a few blocks away on the "Aryan"— what the Nazis called their "master race"—side.

"My husband doesn't know I am here," she admitted. "The Gestapo are everywhere, so it is dangerous. But I had to see how you were doing."

"What are the Gestapo?" Simon asked.

"They are the German political police. They are little more than thugs. They drag people into their headquarters if they think they are helping the Jews or working against Germany. Then they beat them and torture them until the prisoners give them names of other people."

She looked around the tiny apartment sadly while she answered. "I brought you this," she said, handing Mrs. Gorski a *fluden,* a rich fruitcake with nuts and raisins. Simon's mother cut it into tiny squares, and each day they

all had a piece. Simon had a feeling it would be a long time before he had another.

In November, only a month after Simon's family had been forced into the ghetto, the Germans ordered that a wall be built around the ghetto. It had to be paid for and built by Jewish workers. Simon watched the wall going up with a growing sense of dread. When it was completed, ten feet high with barbed wire on the top, the Jewish people were sealed in.

"Now the Poles don't have to watch us starve to death," Mr. Gorski said, staring blankly out into the street.

It became more and more difficult to get food. Polish farmers who had sold them food before were now forbidden to by the Nazis. It was impossible to get meat, eggs, and milk. The only foods available were potatoes, flour, onions, and barley. Many people lived with eight or nine people in a room, and the streets were filled with people dying of starvation. Disease swept through the ghetto, spread by fleas and lice. Delousing stations were set up, but the problem continued.

Mr. Gorski was marched out of the gate every morning with the other workers. Every evening he came home exhausted from sweeping streets or shoveling snow.

Somehow they made it through the winter. They kept telling each other that things would get better. As spring arrived in 1941, it was difficult to get news in the ghetto,

but they knew Hitler had invaded other countries in Europe. Some people believed that America might enter the war. But others said America would not get involved in a European war.

Simon's family huddled together in the cold winter, sleeping on the floor in the tiny kitchen, wrapped in every blanket they possessed. They sweltered in the summer that followed. The Germans ordered that all the schools and libraries be closed. Simon's parents taught him at home, although they had found a tutor for Jozef. Mrs. Gorski supervised Simon's lessons. Hunger had made her listless and her once attractive blond hair was nearly gray. Simon found it difficult to study when his mind was always on the gnawing hunger in his stomach. Mr. Gorski occasionally brought home a bag of potatoes bought from the smugglers who had a thriving business in spite of the danger. But there was never enough to take Simon's mind off the pain in his stomach.

The German soldiers patrolled outside the wall. Inside the ghetto, the Jewish police enforced, sometimes brutally, all German restrictions. The Jewish police enforced the curfew. From the start, Jews had not been allowed to leave their homes from 8:00 P.M. until 8:00 A.M. Anyone found on the streets during those hours was arrested and could be shot. Most people hated the Jewish police, although Simon's mother said most of them did it to provide for their own families.

"I saw one of them shoot a boy about Simon's age who was trying to climb over the fence," Jozef said.

Mrs. Gorski turned her face away and did not answer.

Many of the men who had worked outside the gates were transported to labor camps. But Mr. Gorski managed to get work at one of the small factories set up to aid the German war effort. The Germans had cut the ration cards to about three hundred calories per day, less than a fourth of what a person needed to keep from starving. Mr. Gorski was sometimes given food at work, which he brought home to share. Still, there were days when Simon could hardly drag himself out of bed in the morning because he was so weak. When winter arrived again, Simon's frail, thin body struggled to keep warm. The cold, dark nights grew darker and longer.

*****

One night, in April 1942, Simon heard gunfire a few blocks away. In the morning, the ghetto residents gathered in silent groups. Truckloads of soldiers and SS had dragged about sixty men out of their homes and shot them in the street. Fifty-two people died. People began to refer to it as the "bloody night," and rumors of deportation to concentration camps began to circulate.

*****

On a hot July afternoon, Simon sat with Jozef on the stairs of their apartment building. The streets, as usual, were

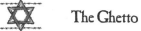

crowded and there were two dead bodies lying on the sidewalk. Simon thought about the first time that he had seen a dead body after the initial bombing and how horrified he had been. Now it was so common that he didn't even flinch. Some people still arranged a funeral and burial in the Jewish cemetery when someone died. But most people could not afford it. They simply put their loved ones out in the street, where they were picked up by wagons and dumped in a mass grave.

Simon's friend Abram came and sat down beside them.

"I wish we could find a place to play soccer," Abram finally said.

Simon shook his head. "I'm too hungry. Running around makes it worse."

"We used to get these pastries from the bakery near our house. They had thick white frosting on them, sometimes chocolate," Abram said dreamily.

"It just makes it worse to think about it," Jozef said. "I am going back inside to study."

When Jozef left, Abram said, "There was a sign posted near my apartment saying that anyone who volunteered for labor would get a loaf of bread and a jar of jam. Some people are so hungry they accepted. I heard they loaded six thousand people onto trains at the *Umschlagplatz*. That's the place where they gather the people who are going east on the train. It's surrounded by a wooden fence and it is right next to the freight train station. There are some buildings there. Someone told me that before the ghetto there was a hospital and a homeless shelter there. Now the Germans are using it to check papers. I heard the Germans built a brand-new camp named Treblinka."

"Maybe it wouldn't be so bad. Working hard is better than starving," Simon said.

Abram sighed. "They took really old people and some little children."

They were silent for a few minutes, thinking about that. "I saw a poster telling parents to give up their children. It sounded like they would be in the country with fresh air and food," Simon said. "Maybe they are sending the old people there, too."

Finally, Abram said, "The smugglers will give you food for helping deliver their stuff."

"The soldiers shoot smugglers," Simon said. "Last week some boys climbed over the fence and were caught. The soldiers shot them. They were younger than us."

Abram shrugged. "We don't have to leave the ghetto. I'm going to do it. My mother is too sick to work, so we won't get any more rations."

After Abram left, Simon went back inside. Jozef was studying at the small kitchen table. Anya was sitting on the mattress in the corner of the kitchen where she slept, playing with her favorite doll. She looked up and gave

Simon a wan smile before she returned to her make-believe world. For a second, Simon was envious of her innocence. Everyone in the family tried to shield Anya from knowing what was really happening. Before the war she had often pestered Simon, begging him to play with her or to take her to the park. He realized she never did that anymore. Now she mostly talked to her doll in a quiet whisper. She never asked to go out. Maybe Anya knew much more than they thought.

chapter three

Smugglers

July 1942

Several days later Simon followed Abram as he pushed his way through the throngs of people crowding the street. He tried not to look guilty as he ducked around men in threadbare suits striding purposefully about their own business. Other people simply stood about as though not sure where to go, and still others sat on the sidewalk, begging for a handout. All the people he passed had the same hollow-eyed look of desperation. Simon was already having second thoughts. He tried not to think about how his parents would react if they knew what he was doing.

He was lagging behind. "Hurry," Abram called, waiting impatiently for him to catch up. As soon as he did, Abram led the way down Franciszkańska Street to the start of Kozla Alley. As poor and rundown as the area where Simon lived was, this was even worse. Decayed buildings with crooked stairways hung over the narrow pavement. Between the

forlorn shop buildings were a few five-story houses. Before the war, they had probably been apartments for laborers. But now they were crowded with people ordered out of the nearby small towns by the Nazis.

The alley came to an abrupt end at the wall that bordered the ghetto. Above the wall, Simon could see the upper floors of houses on the Aryan side. Kozla Alley was far from deserted, however. Vendors' carts stacked with potatoes, beets, and carrots, and stands with loaves of bread and tins of milk filled every space. Several bicycle rickshaws, an idea borrowed from the Chinese, were lined up close to part of the wall. A rickshaw was a seating compartment attached to a bicycle so that it could be pulled through the streets. Simon saw a woman hide a large package under the seat. Then she climbed in, and the man pulling the rickshaw pedaled his way out of the narrow alley and into the ghetto streets.

Many of the men in the alley looked hard and rough, but Abram pushed past them without hesitation. He had been working for the smugglers for several weeks. Until now, however, Simon had resisted when Abram urged him to come with him.

Then yesterday he had waited in line with his mother to pick up their rations. When it was their turn, there was hardly anything left but a little flour, an onion, and a few potatoes. Later, he had seen Abram hurrying home with a

small sack of food. Abram showed him that he had a cabbage, some eggs, and—best of all—two bright red apples. Simon had told him that he would go with him the next day.

Abram boldly approached a tall, dark-haired man. "We are here," he said. The man did not look much older than Jozef. Smuggling was a young man's business, it seemed. Simon thought that before the war the young man probably would have been a trucker or a construction worker. He fixed Simon with a long, hard stare. "This is your friend? He doesn't look very strong."

Simon stood up straight. "I *am* strong," he said.

The man nodded. "We shall see. I am Rubin. You know what to do?"

Simon nodded. Abram had already explained. They would be given packages to deliver to the few people in the ghetto who still had money. They were to bring the payment for the packages back to Rubin. Then at the end of the day, they would be paid. "Watch for the Jewish police. If they catch you, say a man was running and dropped the packages." Rubin shrugged. "Better yet, don't let them catch you."

Simon watched as a man appeared at a barred window on the other side of the high wall that enclosed the ghetto. He worked a small trough between the bars. Below him one of the smugglers held an open burlap bag. The man in the window poured barley into the trough. In a few

moments, the sack was filled. Rubin looked at a list. "You know where this is?" he asked, showing them an address.

The boys nodded. It was not very far. Rubin handed them another sack with a few potatoes and carrots. "Bring the money straight back," he said grimly.

They took turns carrying the heavy sack. At each corner one of them went ahead, searching for German SS and police officers or the Jewish police. They skirted around the bodies along the sidewalks and gutters waiting for the death wagon to take them for burial. It was warm and some of the bodies had started to decompose. The smell on the street was horrific, and Simon tried not to breathe too deeply. Two young, emaciated girls were huddled against a doorway. Simon reached into the sack for a carrot, but Abram grabbed his arm. "They are counted. Rubin will not give us work if we cheat him."

The girls were so infested with lice that Simon could see them crawling on their thin, frail bodies. He backed away; lice had become a terrible problem with so many people crammed together and with a shortage of soap and water. Simon looked away from the girls' pleading eyes. A year ago, or even a few months ago, he would have been devastated by such a sight. But there was so much death around him that it was hard to mourn for strangers.

They found the address, and Abram did the special knock that Rubin had showed him. *Tap, tap, a pause, and three more.* A man opened the door and grabbed the bags with one hand, and with the other hand he shoved some bills into Simon's hands and then quickly shut the door. The whole transaction had taken only a few seconds and not a word was exchanged. Simon hid the money in his shoe and they raced back to Rubin.

Ten more times they raced through the ghetto, delivering packages. "You have done very well," Rubin said when they returned the last time. He gave them each a sack with four potatoes, three small beets, two carrots, a small pack of flour and another of sugar, a small jar of jam, and an even smaller piece of chicken. It was more food than Simon had seen in weeks. Holding up his hand for them to wait, Rubin walked over to one of the stands and selected two red apples and two pieces of taffy candy. "Since it is your first day," he said, adding it to their packs. "Come back tomorrow."

After thanking Rubin, the boys headed home. "Ask your brother Jozef to help us tomorrow and we can get even more," Abram said as they started for home.

"Father insists that Jozef finish his schooling," Simon said. "He would make me go too if there was a teacher close by."

Simon clutched his bag, trying to hide it. Simon had overheard his father saying that there were four or five thousand people dying of starvation every month. Many of the older street boys would not hesitate to beat him up and take his precious food. But today Simon was fortunate. None of the tough, older boys who usually hung around their street were there.

Mr. Gorski was standing in front of the apartment, anxiously looking up and down the street. When he saw Simon, he looked relieved and angry at the same time.

"Where have you been?" he demanded. "Your mother has been frantic. She thought you had been caught in a roundup and sent to that new work camp, Treblinka."

Once, Simon's father had been a big man. But now his clothes hung loosely on him as though they had been made for a much larger man. Simon's clothes hung on him, too, although his pants were several inches too short. In spite of the hunger, he had grown taller.

Abram hurried to the next block, where he lived, and Simon followed his father into the house. His mother's eyes were swollen and red, but before she could speak, Simon dumped his hoard of food on the table. His little sister Anya gasped at the sight of the red apple. It had been months since they had seen any fruit.

Jozef arrived from school before anything was said. The Germans had ordered that all the schools in the ghetto be closed, but former teachers conducted schools secretly in their homes. Only a few students went to each one so as

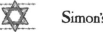

not to arouse suspicion. His eyes widened when he saw the food on the table.

"Did you leave the quarter?" Simon's father asked finally.

Simon shook his head. "No, Father. I just delivered food inside it."

"Smuggled food," Mr. Gorski said. "The Germans would shoot you for that."

"The smugglers pay off the guards," Simon said. "They pretend like they don't see."

Simon's mother cut up the potatoes, chicken, and onion and made soup. With part of the flour she made biscuits, spreading some of the jam on them. It was the best meal that Simon's family had eaten in months and they fell to it eagerly.

"Eat slowly," Mrs. Gorski said. "It will make you feel fuller."

"But it is so good," Anya said between bites. "Almost as good as one of Lydia's dinners."

Everyone laughed, one of the first laughs they had shared in weeks.

Simon looked at his mother. Her parents were living in America in a place called New York, where they reported little antisemitism, or hatred of Jews. They had been rich, and Simon's mother had always had servants and never had

to work. And yet she had remained strong through the whole ordeal, learning to cook, keeping the small apartment as clean as she could, and never complaining, although Simon had heard her muffled sobs at night.

"There is a new factory starting on the next block," Mr. Gorski said to his wife. "It might be wise for you to get a job there. The Germans are taking people with no work permits off the streets."

Mrs. Gorski looked alarmed. "What about Anya?"

"Maybe Mrs. Goldberg next door could watch her while you're at work. It would mean extra food for us if you work."

Mrs. Goldberg was an older woman who lived with her son and daughter in the next apartment. She often came over to visit.

Mrs. Gorski nodded thoughtfully. "I will ask her about it tomorrow."

After dinner, Anya helped her mother clean up the kitchen. Simon read his book. Although the Germans had closed all the libraries, many people had donated books to stock secret libraries around the quarter. Mr. Gorski insisted that Simon read for an hour each day. In addition, he taught him math and science so that when the schools opened again, he would not be far behind. Now that he was home, Simon realized how tired he was from the many trips to deliver the smuggled food. A few years before he could have run all day, but now his body was frail and he tired easily. His eyelids drooped.

Jozef poked Simon with his elbow and grinned when Simon jumped. "Was it scary?" he whispered.

Simon shook his head. "It was like a game."

Jozef was silent for a minute. The grin fell from his face. "It's a game that the penalty for losing is death."

chapter four

Treblinka

Afew days later, Simon went back to
Kozla Alley with Abram. His father still
did not like the idea, but he did not forbid him to go. His mother had been crying before he left.
She gripped his arm so tightly it hurt. "Be careful," she
whispered fiercely in his ear. Then she patted his head and
smiled, keeping up a light appearance for Anya's sake.

"I'm glad you are back," Abram said. "Rubin would
not let me go by myself. He made me help an old man. His
name was Alexander, and he gave me all the heavy sacks to
carry."

When they arrived at the alley, the noise was subdued
and few of the carts had any food. "What happened?"
Abram asked one of the vendors.

"There were two different guards last night who had not
been paid off. They confiscated nearly a ton of food. Two
of our men were caught outside the gate and were shot, and
also two men in the Polish resistance. Some of the Poles are

trying to organize a fighting group. I heard there are already some resistance fighters hiding in the forests—they call them partisans. The men who were shot were meeting to see about smuggling guns into the ghetto."

Rubin pointed to several burlap bags and gave the boys the address. The sacks were heavy, and when they were out of sight, Abram peeked in. Each sack had several tins of milk in addition to flour, sugar, and honey. This time they delivered them to a small bakery that supplied the ration bread. The baker gave them each a small sweet roll he had hidden under a counter. They gobbled up their unexpected treat, licking every crumb off their fingers and moaning with delight. On the way back to Rubin, they rounded a corner and nearly bumped into two SS officers.

Simon still had the baker's money in his pocket. His heart started beating so hard and fast he feared the men could hear it. Abram, however, started cheerfully talking about a soccer game. The SS gave them a long stare but went on with their conversation. Then, just as they reached an alley and Simon allowed himself to breathe again, one of the SS men shouted, "You boys. Halt!"

"Run!" Abram said as they rounded the corner into the alley. Leading the way, he squeezed through a fence and, with Simon right behind, crossed a small courtyard. Simon could hear the heavy tread of the soldiers' boots as he and Abram slipped through a door into the next building.

The two boys raced up several flights of stairs, finally reaching a small door leading out onto the roof. They could still hear the soldiers several flights below them as they crossed the roof and leaped onto the roof of the next building, which was only a short jump away. Trying to stay hidden, they crossed that roof and found a door inside. Luckily, it was unlocked, and they leaped through, locking it from the inside. They clattered down the stairs. Abram peeked through the front door. "Come on," he panted. "I know a place to hide."

Simon's throat was raw from breathing so hard, and there was a pain in his side. They crossed the street, trying not to run and draw attention. They squeezed through another narrow alleyway, and Abram led the way up a wooden fire escape to a small loft. "I hope it's not locked," Abram muttered as he rattled the door handle. It opened, and the boys fell inside.

Simon sank to the floor, trying to catch his breath, while Abram leaned against the door, panting. After a moment, he peeked out the tiny window.

"Good," he said. "They don't know we crossed the street. They are looking on the other side."

Simon got up and stood next to Abram, watching through the grimy window. They could see the SS officers walking up the street, looking in the narrow spaces between buildings and looking up at the rooftops. After a few minutes, they seemed to give up.

"We had better wait awhile," Abram said. He took off his shirt to reveal another in a different color underneath. Then he took his hat off and turned it inside out. When he was done he looked entirely different. "It is a trick Rubin taught me," he explained. He gave his hat to Simon and put Simon's hat on his own head.

Simon looked around the room. It was tiny and filled with boxes. "My cousin used to live here," Abram said. "It's used mostly for storage, but we played here when I visited."

They waited for what seemed to be nearly an hour before venturing back outside. Abram put the money inside his shoe and they walked several blocks out of their way to get back to Kozla Alley. They found Rubin steaming. "Where have you been?" he demanded. His scowl softened when they handed him the money, and he listened while they explained about the narrow escape.

"Are you sure you were not followed?" he asked nervously, scanning the crowd.

Abram told him how they had waited in the loft and taken a long route back.

"Good thinking," Rubin said, nodding, with a thin smile.

Because of the delay they were not able to do as many runs that day. Rubin, however, was in a generous mood.

He filled their packs with the usual potatoes and carrots, but also two tins of milk and, even more wonderful, a half of a plump chicken.

Simon continued going to the alley each day. The little bit of food he brought home every day kept the family from joining the faceless beggars on the streets. But it was still not enough to stop the gnawing hunger pains in Simon's stomach. Still, he knew others were not so fortunate. Dogs and cats had long disappeared from the ghetto, although the rats seemed to have multiplied and grown bolder. Abram told Simon that some people in his building were catching the rats to eat. Every day, the wagons picked up the bodies of those who had starved, and there were even more now because an epidemic was sweeping the city. Every day there were hundreds of bodies buried in unmarked mass graves in the Jewish Cemetery.

One morning, Jozef left for his classes as usual, but in only a few minutes he returned.

"Mr. Michelowski sent me home. He says that nearly everyone on his block has typhus. He is not feeling well himself."

Mrs. Gorski looked alarmed, but Jozef had even worse news. He looked around. "Where is Anya?"

"She is in the kitchen, playing with her doll," Mr. Gorski answered.

Jozef lowered his voice so she could not hear. "Mr. Michelowski says that a few people have escaped from the roundups and made their way back. They say the people that are being shipped out are not going to work camps. They said Treblinka is like a camp for killing Jews."

"That can't be true," Mrs. Gorski said, shaking her head in horror. "Even the Nazis would not be that cruel."

"Mr. Michelowski thinks that it is true. He heard that some of the first people were stuffed into trucks and gassed. They packed them in so tightly they couldn't move. That was too slow for the SS, so now they have developed more efficient means. They gas the people and then burn the bodies in giant crematoria. They say you can smell the burning bodies for miles around the camp. They are even killing babies and little children."

Mr. Gorski sat down heavily and put his head in his hands. "Some parents even sent their children, thinking they would have good food and clean country air. We should have known the Nazis would not be kind to Jewish children."

"Mr. Michelowski thinks the only way to be safe is to have a work permit for one of the factories making things for the German war effort," Jozef said. "They may keep the ones who are working in the factories alive."

Simon's mother had been trying to get a work permit, but there were long lines every day at the council office.

"They just keep saying to come back tomorrow," she said wearily.

Mr. Gorski put his arms around her. "I know a few people on the council. I'll go tomorrow and see what I can do. We need to get you a work permit soon."

Anya was standing by the window, looking out. "Where are all those people going?" she asked.

Simon looked out to see long lines of people, each carrying small satchels of belongings. German soldiers with guns prodded them along. The soldiers ordered them to halt, and Simon could see they were being counted and then separated into columns. Men were being torn from their families and forced into one line. Women with babies and children were put in another row.

As Simon's family watched, a woman carrying a baby suddenly broke loose from the line and started to run. Several shots rang out and the woman fell dead in the street. Mrs. Gorski pulled Anya away from the window before she could see. But Simon continued to watch, horror twisting knots in his stomach. A soldier killed the baby, too.

The lines were moving toward the *Umschlagplatz,* where Simon knew they would be loaded into freight cars. There were hundreds of prisoners, maybe thousands. His mind was too numb to estimate. He saw several boys whom he had known from school. He suddenly sucked in his breath; Abram and his mother were among the prisoners.

chapter five

Missing

M r. Gorski left early the next morning to apply for a work permit for his wife. At eight o'clock curfew, he still had not returned. Simon's mother paced the tiny living space, wringing her hands and crying. Jozef put his arms around her. "Father probably could not get home before curfew. Maybe he is just staying with someone he knows."

Mrs. Gorski wiped her eyes and her face brightened. "You are probably right. Your father always says I worry too much. I am sure he will be home in the morning."

Simon's father did not return the next day or the day after that. Jozef went out to ask if anyone had seen him, but no one had. Jozef sat next to his mother at the small table.

"There was a roundup two days ago. A big one. The council was ordered to provide at least six thousand people. The Jewish police helped round them up. They took them to the train station. A man told me they stuffed them into filthy cattle cars like they were animals," he said bitterly.

"The man said it was hot and the people were crying out, begging for water, but the guards just ignored them."

Mrs. Gorski sat alone by the window for three days, barely rousing herself long enough to prepare the food Simon brought back.

"Where is Papa?" Anya asked over and over again.

"He went away to work," Simon told her.

"When is he coming back?" Anya persisted.

"I don't know," Simon said. "He had to go very far away. On a train. He may be gone a long time."

"He forgot to say good-bye," Anya said as tears formed in the corners of her eyes.

"The train left very early in the morning," Jozef said.

After Simon's father had been missing for four days, Mrs. Gorski seemed to rouse herself. Her eyes were red and puffy from weeping, and her hair looked dull and lifeless. She put on her scarf to go out. "I am going to get a work permit," she said with fierce determination.

Simon had planned to take Jozef to see Rubin, but Mrs. Goldberg was sick and they agreed it was not safe to leave Anya alone. Simon had to work with another runner, a girl named Rutka. He had seen her once before, talking with Rubin. Rutka was thin and her clothes were ragged. However, her dark brown hair was long and curly, and he thought that her eyes were beautiful—like the color of a summer sky. Now that he found himself working with her,

he became suddenly tongue-tied. He had never liked any of the giggly girls at school, preferring to play soccer with his friends. In fact, he had never talked to any girls much except for Anya and his mother.

Rutka's eyes narrowed. "What are you staring at?" she demanded.

"N-nothing," Simon stammered. "I was just surprised."

Rutka put her hand on her hip and scowled. "Surprised at what? That I am a girl?"

"I didn't know that girls did this," he admitted. "But mostly I am surprised that you are so pretty."

A deep red flush crept up Rutka's face, but Simon thought she looked pleased at the compliment. "Let's go," she said gruffly, bending to pick up one of the heavy sacks. Simon leaped to help her, but Rutka pushed him away so hard he toppled to the ground.

"Why did you do that?" Simon sputtered as he scrambled to his feet. Pretty or not, Simon decided that he did not like this ill-tempered girl.

Rubin, who had been watching, gave a loud guffaw. "Rutka doesn't like to be reminded that she's a girl. Do you, Rutka?"

Rutka stood up, straining under her load. Ignoring Rubin, she turned to Simon and said, "I don't need help from a puny thing like you." She started off at a fast pace,

leaving Simon scrambling to pick up his load. The sound of Rubin's laughter followed him as he hurried after her.

Rutka was fearless, and she knew every part of the ghetto. She scurried through alleys and zipped through courtyards, even cutting through buildings, to get to their destinations. It was a hot August day, and Simon was sweating as he struggled to keep up, but the heat did not seem to bother Rutka. He had to admit that her way was safer because they stayed mostly off the streets, where they might run into Nazi officers or the Jewish police.

Late in the afternoon, they arrived at a four-story apartment house not far from one of the heavily guarded gates. The building was ominously quiet, making them hesitate before they walked up to the second floor. There was a boy sitting on the stairs going to the third floor.

"They're all gone," he said dully.

"What do you mean?" Simon asked. "Gone where?"

"The Nazis have a quota. We are not dying fast enough. They just came in and gave everyone five minutes to pack a bag. They marched them all to the train station."

Simon stared at the boy in horror. For weeks, the Germans had been taking people off the streets, but now they had emptied a whole building?

"My sister lived upstairs with her husband and four children. My grandparents lived with them. They are all gone."

Rutka was the first to recover after hearing the boy's story. "Stay here with the food. I'll see if I can sell it."

She dashed outside, returning a few minutes later with several men, who quickly divided the sacks and left.

At the door she turned back to the young boy and, with a surprising show of sympathy, asked, "Do you have somewhere to go?"

The boy nodded. "I live with my parents, not far from here. They don't know yet. How am I going to tell my mother what happened?"

Simon did not tell his mother about the empty building. It was late when she returned. She had gotten her permit and started work that same day. Dark circles had formed under her eyes. She looked tired and defeated. Jozef made her a cup of tea from a small packet Rubin had given Simon. Simon cut up a potato that she cooked with a tin of milk to make potato soup.

"Was it awful?" Simon asked.

Mrs. Gorski forced a smile. "There are huge stacks of clothing. The good things I suppose will be sent back to Germany. My job is to remove buttons and hooks from the raggedy clothing. Then I divide by color, cut strips of cloth, and wind them into balls. They will be made into rugs. Some of the material is crawling with lice." She shuddered. "I will get used to it," she said briskly. "I imagine the first day of any job is hard."

Simon felt a surge of pride as he watched his mother stir the soup.

"We are a stronger people than Mr. Hitler thinks," he said.

"Who is Mr. Hitler?" Anya asked, looking up from the doll dress she was trying to sew from a scrap of cloth.

"He's just a bad man," Mrs. Gorski said. "Nothing for you to worry about."

Anya looked up at her mother. "Is he the man who wants to kill all the Jews?"

There was a moment of stunned silence. They had all tried so hard to keep Anya from knowing.

"Where did you hear that?" Mrs. Gorski gasped.

Anya pointed to the thin partition that separated them from the two families that lived next door. "I heard the neighbors talking when I was in bed."

Simon's mother wrapped her arms around Anya. "Don't worry. They say as long as you have a work permit, you are all right. The Nazis need our labor."

"We should fight them," Jozef said angrily.

Simon looked at his brother. His dark hair was unkempt and he impatiently brushed it out of his eyes with his hand. He too had grown taller, although he was so thin his face looked pinched. Simon looked like his mother, but he thought Jozef looked more like his father every day.

Mrs. Gorski shook her head. "How can we? We are not soldiers and we have no weapons. Half of us are old or are children, and many are sick. All of us are starving. How can we fight a well-trained, well-equipped army? Perhaps England will free us, or the Americans. I heard the Americans are fighting now, too. If we can just survive a bit longer, someone will help us. The world cannot ignore such evil."

"Some men in the ghetto are organizing a fighting force," Jozef whispered that night, as they lay on their thin mattress, trying to sleep in the sweltering apartment. "They are calling it the Jewish Fighting Organization, or ZOB." A few feet away Simon could hear his mother's even breathing as she slept. Jozef leaned up on one elbow. "I'm going to try to join them."

"You are only fifteen," Simon whispered back. "They will not let you join."

"I'll tell them I am older. The Nazis are not taking me without a fight," Jozef said fiercely.

Simon had trouble sleeping that night. He thought about Jozef's desire to fight. Before the war, Jozef had been a gentle, studious boy who had to wear glasses because of his weak eyes—not the sort of person to be a fighter. But Jozef was also determined and not afraid to fight if he thought a wrong was being done. It had always been Jozef who came to Simon's aid when bigger boys picked on him at school.

At school, Simon had been the class clown, often in trouble with his teachers. Simon knew he had grown up some since the war began, but he was not sure he would have the courage to fight even if he had the chance.

Simon tried to say a prayer for his father, but then he shook his head, rubbing his eyes with his fists. What kind of a God would allow such things to happen? And even if God would not protect his people, how could any human being allow such things to happen? It was Hitler's orders, but what about the hundreds of people who followed those orders? And what about the thousands of people who knew what was happening and did nothing? Even worse, what about all the people who were glad it was happening? He was still awake when he heard his mother setting on some water to boil for tea. It was still dark, but she had to leave for work. He stumbled out of bed to see her before she left.

"You look terrible," she said, feeling his head for fever.

"I couldn't sleep," he admitted.

"You stay home with Anya today," she said. "Let Jozef go in your place."

Simon sat at the table, sipping weak tea until daybreak. He woke Jozef and told him where to find Rubin.

"Be careful," Simon said as Jozef stepped out the door. Jozef looked for any sign of the SS and started off.

"If you work with Rutka, don't try to help her, do you understand?" Simon called after him.

chapter six

A Daring Plan

Jozef could not stop talking about Rutka that night. "She is the bravest girl I've ever met," he said with admiration in his voice.

Simon was astounded. "You *like* her?"

Jozef nodded. "She is very pretty, too, don't you think?"

Simon shrugged, as if he had not noticed. "I think she is a very disagreeable girl," he said.

"She is *fierce*. I like that," Jozef said.

The next day, when it was Simon's turn to work with Rutka, she was almost friendly. "Does your brother have a girlfriend?" she asked as they started out.

Simon shook his head. "Mostly he just studies when he is home."

"Do you think he likes me?" she asked, sounding almost shy.

"He said you were pretty," Simon admitted. He could see that this pleased her. She reached with her free hand, absently fluffing her hair in an uncharacteristically girlish gesture.

After Simon and Rutka had finished their deliveries for the day, they turned down a street that was normally crowded with people. Today, however, it was almost empty. Suddenly, Simon reached out and grabbed her arm, pulling her into the recessed doorway of a deserted shop. Anger flashed across her face and she started to shake him loose. Then she saw the reason. Two Jewish policemen were standing across the street. They appeared to be having an argument of some sort, and Simon hoped that they had not noticed them. He twisted the doorknob, and, to his relief, it opened.

Inside, they saw that the store had been looted of everything. Empty shelves lined the long, narrow room, and the floor was covered with broken glass and litter. Rutka had recovered from her shock and ran to the back, looking for another door. There was a small workroom and a broken door leading to a narrow alley. They ran down it and several other connecting alleys before finally stopping to catch their breath.

Rutka looked at Simon and actually smiled. "You saved us. I guess you are a good partner after all." She leaned back against a building and peered down the deserted alley. "Have you noticed how few people there are?" She reached into a pocket and pulled out a smashed piece of bread. She divided it, handing half to Simon.

Simon accepted the bread gratefully.

"The Nazis are going to keep on until we are all dead," she said matter-of-factly.

"People with work permits will be safe," Simon said.

"For now," she said darkly. "You should try to escape. You could pass for Polish. You are blond, and you speak Polish well." She sighed. "So many of our people only speak Yiddish."

"You speak Polish just as well," Simon said.

Rutka shrugged. "I speak both. My father was Polish and my mother was Jewish. They were both killed on the first day of the bombing. I might try to escape one day."

Simon shook his head. "I wouldn't leave my family."

"If you ever do escape, don't trust any of the Poles. They are as bad as the Germans. They were glad when we were shoved into this ghetto. They turn Jews in for rewards. I heard one say he could always tell a Jew. He said he could smell them." She snorted. "I was standing right next to him when he said it."

"Why do people hate us so much?" Simon asked.

Rutka shrugged and pushed herself away from the wall. "Some of the people believe in the so-called blood libels— false rumors that Jews sacrificed Christian children and used their blood for rituals."

Simon stared at her. "How could they believe such a terrible thing?"

"Ignorance and centuries of prejudice. We had better get back. Rubin will be worried."

Simon looked at Rutka. She was only a year older than he was, but she knew so much. He wondered if she had been a scholar like Jozef before the war.

Rutka continued talking as they walked. "My father said that his parents believed all kinds of terrible things about the Jews. They disowned him when he married my mother."

Simon was so wrapped up in his thoughts that he had almost reached Rubin's stall before he realized that something was dreadfully wrong. Rutka held up her hand to keep him from stumbling closer. The alley was littered with overturned carts and smashed food. Several bodies were in the street, lying in widening pools of blood.

Rutka grabbed the arm of another runner as he walked by them. "What happened?"

"The SS and Jewish police came. You had better get away from here," he said.

"Did you see Rubin?" Simon asked.

"They took him away with the others. The SS arrested about twenty people and took them to the Jewish police station. They will all be shot," the man answered before he hurried away.

Simon and Rutka walked quickly away from the alley. A few blocks from Simon's apartment, Rutka stopped and

ducked into the doorway of a large, empty building. She divided the money that they had received from their delivery. She also handed him a folded piece of paper. "Give this to Jozef," she said. With a quick wave, she was gone.

Jozef's face looked grim when Simon told him what had happened. He looked at the note from Rutka and pocketed it without comment.

"How are we going to get food?" Simon whispered, so that Anya did not hear.

Jozef shrugged. "At least we have some money. I will talk with Rutka tomorrow. We can figure something out."

As soon as it was light the next morning, Simon slipped out. He made his way to the Jewish police station and hid in the shadows of a doorway across the street. After a time, the door opened and the prisoners were marched out. Rubin was among them. His eyes met Simon's, but he did not react. The Jewish police made them line up against a brick wall. Simon was suddenly aware that Rutka was beside him. She took his hand. "We shouldn't watch," she said.

Simon nodded, but they remained where they were. Some of the men were pleading for their lives, but Rubin stood stoically, awaiting his fate. Suddenly, the sharp crack of gunfire rang out. Rubin fell like a stone, dead instantly. Beside Simon, Rutka sighed softly. "The police are Jews," she said.

"My mother says if they don't do what the Germans say, their own families are killed."

"How did the world get so awful?" Rutka asked.

"Maybe it always was, and we just didn't notice," Simon answered.

Rutka nodded before she slipped away.

Simon walked slowly home. Once inside the apartment, he cut a piece of their last loaf of rye bread for Anya, but she looked at it and would not eat. "I don't feel good," she said. She curled up on her mattress in the corner of the kitchen.

Simon felt her head. She was burning with fever. He wet some rags and washed her face to cool it. "My head hurts," she mumbled.

When Mrs. Gorski returned home, she knelt beside her daughter. Tears streamed down her face. "I think it is typhus. She needs medicine," she sobbed.

"Maybe I can get some," Jozef said.

His mother gave him a questioning look. "I joined the ZOB," Jozef admitted. "They can sometimes get things like that."

Jozef had told Simon that he was helping build underground bunkers and escape tunnels through basements and alleys. The ZOB printed a handbill urging people to fight. "Do they have weapons?" Simon asked.

"A few," Jozef answered. "Not nearly enough. Some of the Polish underground are helping us."

Simon's mother had no choice but to go to work the next morning. She coaxed Anya into swallowing some spoonfuls of thin soup before she left. Jozef left a few minutes later. Simon sat by Anya's bed, dipping rags into cool water and applying them to her body, trying to bring down the fever.

Jozef had only been gone a few hours when he returned. Rutka was with him.

"How is Anya?" he asked.

Simon shook his head. "The same."

"No one has any medicine," Jozef said. "We have asked everyone. Rubin might have been able to get some."

There was dead silence as they thought of Rubin. "Maybe Lydia could help us. She only lives a few blocks away from the wall," Simon said. "I could go there."

Jozef shook his head. "Too dangerous."

"I could do it. Even Rutka said I could pass for Polish," Simon said. "I'm sure Lydia would help us. She loves Anya."

"You can't trust the Poles," Rutka said.

"We can trust Lydia," Simon said.

Rutka shrugged. "I can get you out, but your life may depend on her."

Jozef looked at Anya. Even with the cool rags, she mumbled, incoherent with fever. He nodded reluctantly. "Be careful."

Rutka snapped her fingers. "I have an idea. Do you still have your old school uniform? If we can time it right, you could just be a schoolboy returning home. You could carry some books."

"I think it is in that trunk. My mother was hoping I could return to school." He rummaged through the trunk packed with blankets and found the uniform folded neatly at the bottom. He went to the other room and put it on. The jacket and pants were short; he was surprised at how much he had grown. But because he had lost so much weight, they still fit reasonably well.

Rutka clapped her hands when he returned to the kitchen. "Perfect."

Simon took off the jacket and rolled it up. With a quick wave at Jozef, he followed Rutka out into the street. Walking quickly, she led him down several narrow roads and, not far from the wall, she ducked into an old building. They went down the stairs to a basement and through another door leading into the basement of the next building. They passed through several buildings this way, some with doors, others with small passageways made by removing cement blocks. At last she stopped. "We are actually past the wall now. This building is empty, but be careful when you step outside."

Simon struggled into his jacket. Rutka handed him the book they had brought with them. "I will be waiting for you in the last basement," she said. "Do you know how to get to her house from here?"

Simon nodded. "It is only a few streets over."

He climbed up the stairs, trying to calm his stomach. At the top of the stairs, a moment of panic struck him when he could not open the door. It was only a sticky door handle, however, and after several tries, the door opened with a noisy creak. Simon stood for a moment, fully expecting to see German police standing there alerted by the noise. Hearing nothing, he pushed open the door and stepped through.

chapter seven

Medicine for Anya

The door opened out into an alley. Taking a deep breath to steady himself, Simon walked around the buildings to the street. There was the sound of polka music, and Simon saw an open-air café. His stomach lurched. Sitting at one of the tables were four German soldiers. They were singing along with the music, and the Polish waitress giggled because they were slightly off key. Simon had to walk right past them. He took out his book, pretending to read as he walked along. Perhaps the soldiers would think he was very studious.

A wagon went by, loaded with potatoes and cabbages. No one on the street paid any attention, and why should they? They were all well-fed. Did they know that over the wall, people were dying of hunger? Of course they knew, Simon told himself angrily. They knew, and they didn't care. If anything, they were glad.

Two nuns crossed the street in front of him. They both smiled. Simon remembered one day when he had been walking with a friend from school. The boy was a Pole, and when he had seen nuns, he always greeted them. "Good afternoon, Sisters," Simon said.

"Good afternoon to you," one of them said sweetly. Simon stared after them. Did they know? They seemed so nice. They spent their whole lives serving God, yet they heard the cries of the people starving and dying, and they did nothing.

The soldiers gave him no more than a passing glance as he walked by, and Simon relaxed a little. He walked to Lydia's apartment. He panicked while he waited for his knock to be answered. It had been over a year since he had seen her. What if she had changed? What if she had moved? Just before he lost his courage and ran away, the door opened and a wide-eyed Lydia looked at him.

"Simon? Is that really you?" Looking around nervously, she pulled him into the house and shut the door.

Lydia hugged him, tears flowing down her cheeks. "I can't believe it. What are you doing here? It is very dangerous." Without waiting for a reply, she asked, "How are your mother and father and Jozef? And how is my sweet little Anya?"

"That's why I am here," Simon said. Lydia bustled around the kitchen, making tea and setting out a plate of cookies while he told her about his father's disappearance and Anya's sickness.

"She needs medicine, or she will die," Simon said. "Can you help? I didn't know where else to go."

Lydia looked pale. "Medicines are hard to obtain. The Germans take everything good for their soldiers. I will go to my doctor. He may have something he can give me."

Lydia opened a small closet door. It was full of mops, brooms, and buckets. "My husband would turn you in. Stay in here. I should be back before my husband returns from work, but just in case, stay in here. He would never go into this closet."

Simon turned over a wooden bucket and sat down. Lydia shut the door, and a minute later he heard the front door close. It was dark and stuffy in the closet, and Simon had to fight the panic growing inside him. What if Lydia betrayed him? He knew the Germans rewarded Poles who turned in Jews. The time dragged by slowly. Finally, after several hours, he heard the door open. He started to stand up, but then he realized the footsteps were heavy men's boots.

He heard the sound of water running into a teakettle. His heart was pounding in fear. It must be Lydia's husband home early, Simon thought. He heard the door open again. "You are home early," he heard Lydia say.

"Some supplies didn't come, so the boss sent us home," Simon heard a man's voice answer.

"Why don't you take a shower and then catch a nap while I fix dinner?"

"Maybe I will," he said. They chatted for a few minutes more and then Simon heard the sound of running water. Lydia opened the closet door. She put her finger to her lips and hurried with him out the front door.

"My doctor didn't have any medicine, so he sent me to another. I had to take the tram. The new doctor said there was a new medicine that would help, but he didn't have any. He gave me some aspirin for her fever and a sulfa drug that might help." She tucked a small sack into his pack. Then she gave him two cans of American soup.

"The doctor said to try to get some nourishment into her." She gave him a quick hug. "God be with you," she said as she stepped back through the door and closed it.

Simon was alarmed when he saw how late it was. He hurried back toward the building where he had left Rutka. To his dismay, the soldiers were still at the sidewalk café. One of them said in Polish, "What is your hurry?"

"I went to a friend's house, and now I am going to be late for dinner," Simon said. The lie tumbled out of his mouth, and his voice sounded high and shaky, but the soldier seemed to believe him. Thinking fast, he added, "My mother will be angry."

The soldier laughed. "I know about mothers," he said. His voice was slightly slurred. "You had better run."

Simon forced a smile and started off at a trot. Then, suddenly, a German soldier riding one of those three-wheeled motorcycles roared around the corner. Seeing Simon, he shouted, "Halt! Where are you going, boy?"

Simon froze. There was no way to escape. Slowly, he turned around. Fear churned in his stomach, and he thought he might vomit. Would they shoot him? What if they found the medicine? Would he be strong enough not to betray Lydia?

The soldier climbed off his motorcycle and started toward him. Then a miracle happened. The first soldier called out cheerfully, "Let him go. He is late for dinner, and his mother will box his ears."

Simon forced a sheepish grin and nodded. Laughing, the motorcycle soldier waved him on. "Go on, then."

Simon ran into the alley and slipped in the door. He leaned against it until his heart settled down. Then Simon hurried to the basement and wiggled through the opening.

"I was getting worried," Rutka whispered as she helped him replace the concrete blocks. "Did you get the medicine?"

Simon nodded. "Yes, but we have to hurry. I saw a clock on the café wall. It's almost eight o'clock. We don't want to be out after curfew."

As soon as they reached the ghetto, Rutka headed off for the room where she lived with her aunt and uncle.

Simon raced through the alleys and side streets to his house, reaching it just as his mother arrived home from her job. He gave her the medicine and soup, with a note from Lydia telling her how to administer the medicine.

Simon's mother took the medicine from him. "You left the ghetto? Don't you know how dangerous that is?"

"It was the only way," Simon said. "I was careful."

His mother gave him a quick hug. "That was very brave. But I don't want to lose one child to save another."

His mother heated the soup and coaxed Anya into eating a few bites. She gave her the medicine. Anya's body was covered with a rash and she moaned when her mother applied new cool rags. In the morning, however, her fever was down a little, and after three more days she managed to sit up and play with her doll.

It was almost September and the streets of the ghetto, once so packed with people, were nearly empty. The people without work permits did not dare go out for fear of being caught. Mrs. Gorski made Simon and Jozef promise they would stay hidden in the tiny apartment with Anya. Then, a few nights later, Simon sat up in bed. From not far away came the sounds of screams and sporadic gunfire. His mother was standing at the window. "Now they are even raiding at night," she said.

When they heard the same sounds the following night, she seemed to reach a decision. In the morning she handed Simon and Jozef a pillowcase each and told them to pack a few belongings.

"The Germans are emptying all the buildings. It is not safe here. They would take Anya for sure. Some people are hiding their families at the warehouse. We will go early, before the bosses arrive."

Taking a change of clothes and a small blanket each, they followed their mother through the still-dark streets. Jozef carried Anya. She was better but still very weak. She had insisted on packing her favorite doll.

The warehouse was a huge, cavernous space with rows and stacks of rags piled high. Simon's mother led them to a remote corner. They maneuvered several stacks to make a small space, hidden from anyone walking down the rows. They spread their blankets out on the floor.

"Don't make a sound," Mrs. Gorski warned. "At night the bosses go home and you can move about or even go outside."

"I don't like it here, Mama. Why can't we go home?" Anya whined.

"Look, Anya," Simon said. "It's like a little playhouse. It will be fun staying here."

Anya still looked doubtful, but Simon's mother gave him a grateful look. Jozef threw his bag down in the corner. "I'm sick of hiding."

Mrs. Gorski brushed the hair from Jozef's eyes. "Maybe it won't be that long. Maybe things will change."

"Yes," Jozef said. "They will get worse."

In spite of Jozef's predictions, there were a few months of peace. The deportations seemed to have stopped. Where there had once been four hundred thousand people in the ghetto, now there were only about thirty-five thousand working for the Germans. Jozef told Simon the ZOB thought there were another twenty-five thousand people hidden in underground bunkers and hiding places. Jozef left every night, slipping through the silent streets to the ZOB headquarters on Mila Street. He was helping them build more underground bunkers. Although Simon begged to help, Jozef refused, saying they only took people older than sixteen. With the help of his new friends there, Jozef was able to bring a small amount of food each day. His mother was given a thin bowl of soup and a small piece of dark bread at work each day.

In the daytime, Simon and Jozef slept or read. They exchanged a few books with other families hidden among the stacks of clothes. The warehouse smelled musty and old. Except for the boredom, they were comfortable enough. At night, they could move around and even go outside, hidden by a wooden fence around a shipping dock. But with the onset of winter, it was very cold.

Soldiers occasionally walked through the factory, and once some SS officers came in a surprise raid. The hidden families rolled up their blankets against the stacks and moved quietly up and down the rows, escaping detection.

For four months they managed to hide. Everyone believed that 1943 would be the year the Americans would come and free Poland.

One day, in early January, Jozef said, "Some of the empty apartments still have water and the gas has not been turned off. I'm going to sneak into one and take a bath tomorrow."

"I'll come with you," Simon said. "I haven't had a bath for months."

Simon's mother looked at Jozef. "Do you think it is safe?"

Jozef shrugged. "The soldiers don't usually go back into the buildings they have emptied. We'll be careful."

"All right," Mrs. Gorski agreed. "You two can go tomorrow. Maybe Anya and I will go the next day."

They slipped out early the next morning and hurried up the deserted street, staying close to the silent buildings. Simon shivered. It was cold, but more than that, he felt the weight of all the people who had crowded these streets just a few months before. Now, in all probability, they were dead.

They chose a building not far from the factory. Jozef climbed up the dark staircase. "Let's start with the top apartment. If we hear someone coming, we might have time to go out to the roof and get away."

There were three apartments on the top floor. One was locked, and they could not get in, but the next one they looked at was open. Through the streaks of light coming through the windows from the rising sun, they could see that the occupants had left in a hurry. Bowls with the crusted remains of beet soup were on the table, and a trunk was open, with clothes scattered on the floor.

"Does it make you feel funny being in here?" Simon whispered.

Jozef shrugged. "A little. The people who lived here are probably dead," he said harshly. "They don't care."

He checked the water. It was on, but it was cold. The gas was still on, too, so they rummaged in the kitchen and found a large pot to heat water on the gas stove. A search through the cupboards produced a small scrap of soap. Simon filled the tub and sank in gratefully. "I remember when Mama had to order you to take a bath," Jozef teased.

While Simon scrubbed every inch of himself, Jozef looked through the trunk. "We can wash our clothes," he said. "I found some things we can wear while they dry." He held up a man's shirt and pants. "They are big, but at least they are clean."

Simon emptied the dirty water and Jozef ran a bath for himself. Then they filled the tub again and, using the last of the soap, scrubbed their clothes.

The apartment was small but comfortable. There was a bed in the corner with a real mattress and sheets. It had been a long time since they had slept on anything but a hard floor and a thin blanket. Jozef peered out the window, being careful not to move the curtain.

"It is not safe to go out. I just saw a patrol go by," he said. "Let's spread our clothes out and take a nap while they dry."

Simon nodded. The warm bath had made him sleepy. They curled up on the bed. Who would have ever known that a bath and a comfortable bed could be such a luxury?

The next thing Simon knew, Jozef was shaking him. The room was completely dark. "We slept all day," Jozef said. "Mama will be worrying."

They pulled on their damp clothes. They didn't have a clock, but Simon could tell it was well past sundown. The Germans did not usually patrol much at night, although he and Jozef would still have to watch out for the Jewish police. They ran down the steps and slipped out into the frosty cold. The wind cut through their damp clothes so that in only a few steps, Simon was shaking. Staying close to the empty buildings, they ran to the shipping dock behind the factory and slipped through a loose board in the fence.

Jozef held up his hand. "Something is wrong," he said. "No one is outside."

"Maybe it's just too cold," Simon whispered.

Jozef shook his head. "Someone should be out. Stay here—I'll see if I can find out what is happening."

Simon crouched in the dark shadows of a loading platform. Jozef was gone a long time, and Simon fought a rising tide of panic. What if something happened to Jozef? Then, just when he had almost collapsed with despair, Jozef was back.

"Come on," Jozef said brusquely.

Simon stood up. "Was Mama worried?"

"They're gone," Jozef choked out. "There was only one old man left inside. He said the SS raided the warehouse this afternoon. Somehow he escaped, but everyone else is gone."

chapter eight

Alone

Simon stumbled after his brother. He looked at Jozef in complete disbelief. "What are we going to do?"

Jozef stopped walking. "I don't know," he admitted. "We need to find a place to hide and think."

"Let's try this building," Simon said listlessly. He pointed to a large building in the middle of an empty block.

"Listen," Jozef said.

Simon froze. "I don't hear anything."

"That's what I mean," Jozef said.

"Maybe we are the only ones left alive," Simon said.

"No. There will be others. The ZOB has hiding places. I'll go and find them in the morning."

They chose an apartment on the third floor. It was very dark, but they felt their way to a kitchen table and chairs.

"Maybe Mama and Anya got away," Simon said finally.

"No. They were rounded up like animals and stuffed into cattle cars to be taken away and killed. The Nazis won't be done until they have killed every one of us." He reached into his shirt and pulled something out. "It is Anya's doll. It was on the floor near the front entrance."

Simon's voice broke in a sob. "Poor Anya. She loved that doll." He pounded his fist on the table. "They could have at least let her keep the doll for comfort."

"The Nazis would never do anything to help a Jew, even a little girl," Jozef said.

"Maybe Mama will be put to work in Germany," Simon said hopefully.

Jozef sighed. "Maybe. But not Anya."

They sat through the night, talking a little but mostly just sitting in silence. Neither of them cried. Their sadness was too deep for tears to relieve.

When the first rays of sun peaked through the windows, Jozef stood up. "I'm going to get you out of the ghetto."

Alarmed, Simon looked at his brother. "What about you? I'm not going without you."

"I am going to fight. You are only thirteen. That's too young to fight."

"You are only fifteen," Simon reminded him.

"Almost sixteen," Jozef said. "I have been training with the ZOB. You would just be in the way. Besides, if you don't survive, our family is gone. You have the best chance because you don't look Jewish. You can say you are an orphan. Your parents were killed in the bombing."

Simon shook his head furiously. "Not without you."

Jozef squatted down in front of him. "The ZOB has escape routes. When we have fought all we can, we will get away."

"Then I will fight with you and we will escape together," Simon said stubbornly. "If you make me leave, I'll come back." Simon's voice choked with sadness and anger. "We have to stay together."

Jozef was silent for a few minutes. "I will talk to Mordecai Anielewicz. He is the leader of the ZOB. He is only twenty-four, but he is our commander. He says we are all going to die, but if we fight, at least we can take back some control of our lives and not be herded into their cattle cars like sheep. They will pay dearly to kill us. I will ask him what I should do about you. You wait here until I return."

Simon nodded. "Tell him I can carry messages or help make the bunkers."

The apartment was very cold and there was no heat or water. Simon found some blankets in a closet to wrap around himself. He sat on the bed, rocking himself back and forth, moaning with grief for his mother and Anya. The doll was on the table. Simon picked it up and held it close, weeping into its cotton-stuffed body. Then, suddenly filled with anger, he threw it across the room.

After a time, hunger made him dry his eyes and make a floor-by-floor search of the other apartments, looking for some scrap of food. The occupants had taken everything with them. On the first floor, he found two bodies, shot by the Nazis. Simon stepped over them, trying not to look at the puddles of congealed blood around them. In that kitchen, he found a small loaf of dry bread and a few potatoes. He stuffed some bread into his mouth and took the rest of the food back upstairs.

Suddenly, he heard the sounds of gunfire. It seemed to be coming from the *Umschlagplatz*. The gunshots went on for some time. He looked out the window, but he could not see anything except empty streets. After a while the noise stopped, but Jozef still did not return. Simon paced the floor, trying to decide what to do. How long should he wait? It was getting dark. He sat on a kitchen chair, rocking himself as he tried to think.

At first light he decided to leave, but just then the door flew open and Jozef was there. "We chased them away!" he shouted excitedly.

"What do you mean?" Simon asked.

"When I got to the ZOB headquarters, soldiers were still loading people onto the trains. Some of us infiltrated the lines, and at the signal, we started shooting the soldiers. The people who were left in line ran away and hid."

"Did you see Mama and Anya?" Simon asked with a small surge of hope.

Jozef shook his head. "They were already gone. The Nazis had already shipped out five thousand people, but we saved a lot of people."

"They will be back tomorrow with more soldiers," Simon said.

"Then we will fight them again. We need more guns and weapons. Mordecai gave me a gun today, so I could fight. We got a few weapons from the soldiers we killed, but we still don't have enough."

Later that day, Simon followed Jozef to a hidden bunker under one of the buildings. The young men there were jubilant with victory.

A dark-haired man with weary eyes entered the bunker, and the men were silent. Obviously, this was their leader, Mordecai. He spoke to several of the men and then approached Jozef and Simon. "This is my little brother, Simon," Jozef said.

"I want to fight with Jozef," Simon said, standing up as tall as he could.

Mordecai looked at them. "No," he said shortly. "I will arrange for both of you to escape."

"I can fight," Jozef sputtered. "I did today."

"You did well today," Mordecai said almost gently. "But your brother is only a child and you are not much

more than that. There have been enough children dying. At any rate, I don't have enough guns for the men I already have."

Jozef started to protest, but Mordecai waved his hand. "I have made up my mind. You can stay for now, but when the Germans attack again, you must leave. There are some Polish partisans who will hide you. Maybe you can make your way to Palestine. Jewish people are building a new homeland there on our ancient lands. They will need strong young people."

Three days later, Jozef and Simon were hard at work on a bunker when one of the ZOB fighters burst in. "The Germans attacked near the gates. We managed to fight them off, but a lot of our men were killed."

Simon was stunned. Working hard in the underground bunker, he had not heard the fighting. Jozef was angry that he missed the fight.

"I want to fight," Jozef said to Mordecai. "I am not too young. I can handle a weapon and I can help defeat the Nazis!"

As Jozef continued his impassioned speech, Mordecai exploded. "We are all going to die!" he screamed. "Do you understand? The Germans killed more than a thousand men today. They will never allow us to win. They will be back with tanks and weapons and soldiers. In the end, they will win. All we can do is kill as many as we can before they do.

And then hope that some of us escape and survive. You are going to leave as soon as I can make arrangements."

While Jozef and Simon waited, they helped make more bunkers and tunnels. "I wonder what happened to Rutka," Jozef said one day as they worked.

A man named Janeck, who was working with them spoke. "Are you talking about Rutka who worked for the smugglers? A pretty girl?"

"That's her," Jozef said. "Do you know where she is?"

"She was caught in a roundup," the man said. "I saw her being taken to the trains."

"I heard that she escaped," another man offered. "Someone told me she crawled through a drainpipe."

After Jozef heard that news, he was less resistant to the idea of leaving. "Maybe we can find her," he said, with more life in his voice than Simon had heard in days.

"Is she your girlfriend?" Simon teased.

He expected Jozef to deny this or to possibly punch him in the arm for even suggesting such a thing. They had always been in agreement that girls were silly. But to Simon's amazement, Jozef nodded. "I like her a lot."

Day after day they waited, but the Germans did not attack. The men became bold. "We scared them away. Now that they know we will fight, they are afraid," the men boasted.

Mordecai made them keep working, making a system of tunnels from building to building. "They will be back," he said.

*****

When days and then weeks passed, Simon wondered if Mordecai was wrong. The head of the ZOB drove the men with a feverish intensity, erecting barricades and new bunkers. Simon and Jozef carried messages and instructions. The fighters still did not have enough weapons. They would fight in a hit-and-run fashion, using the tunnels to move around the city.

After a few months, on one April morning, the Germans roared into the ghetto with trucks and soldiers. Simon had been helping build a bunker at the far end of the ghetto, and Jozef was delivering a message to some ZOB members. Simon did not know of the Nazi invasion until Mordecai came to him about noon.

"You can't wait any longer. You must leave now," Mordecai said. "I have made arrangements for you."

Simon put down the sandbag he was carrying. "What about Jozef?"

Mordecai hesitated. "We were taken by surprise. The Nazis managed to capture some of our men. One of the men said Jozef was among them."

Simon sank to the ground. "No! Not Jozef too." He sobbed.

Mordecai knelt down beside him. "Listen to me. The Nazis were dismantling factories and taking out equipment. We think they are going to set up the factories somewhere else. They will need many people to work in the factories. Jozef is young and strong. The Germans are not killing everyone. Those who can work may be saved. Jozef has a chance to survive. Alive or dead, he would want you to escape. He told me that many times. You must live, for him and for the rest of your family."

Simon looked at him, still too shocked to say anything. Mordecai showed him an address. "Remember the address. It is only a few blocks away from the wall. They will be expecting you. They will hide you for a while and then pass you on to others to get you out of the city."

Simon retraced the route he had taken with Rutka. As he ran through the deserted streets of the ghetto, he heard a sound. For a minute, Simon did not recognize it. Then he knew what it was. Tanks. The battle was starting.

The sounds were muffled as he squeezed through the basement passageways. But he could hear the crackle of gunfire as he reached the Aryan side and cautiously opened the door.

The streets were busy. It was as though no one realized a desperate battle was going on, hidden by the ghetto wall.

Farmers' carts rumbled along, heading for the markets, and a few cars rolled past. Trying to blend into the scene, Simon walked briskly, pretending to be on an important errand. He smiled at strangers like he didn't have a care in the world, although his heart was pounding, and he could not stop thinking about his brother.

Simon did not see any soldiers, and no one on the streets gave him a second glance. The street was in a poor section of town. The houses were small and close together. He reached the address he had memorized and knocked softly on the door.

A woman answered. She glanced around nervously, then motioned him in and quickly shut the door.

"You were not noticed?" she asked.

Simon shook his head. "I am sure I was not," he answered.

The woman looked out the window one more time as if to reassure herself. Satisfied, she said shortly, "Come with me."

She led him to a small kitchen. "I am Irena," she said. She pointed to a man sitting at the table. "This is my husband, Dominick." The man nodded. Saying nothing, he cut off hunks of bread and a wedge of cheese for Simon. Then he pulled the firebox of logs from the wall and lifted up a panel to reveal a small, dark room, scarcely bigger than a tiny closet. "You will have to stay in here for now. Tonight I will take you to a safer place."

Simon looked at the dark space fearfully, but Dominick gave him a little push. "It is just for today. Stay quiet. You will be safe here," Dominick said as he slid the panel back into place.

Simon heard the wood box being put back in place. It was utterly dark. He sat on the dirt floor, listening to the sounds above him. After a while he fell asleep, totally exhausted from the day's events.

The smell of food cooking woke Simon sometime later. He had no way to judge how much time had passed.

Now that he was fully awake, Simon could hear the murmur of voices and the clink of dinner dishes. He thought that perhaps the couple had company. He tried to make out words, but the wood muffled the voices. The smell of food from the kitchen made him wish he had saved some of the cheese Dominick had given him.

A few more hours passed before he heard footsteps and the door close. Still, Dominick did not come. Simon's legs were cramped, and he needed to go to the bathroom desperately. He heard Irena's steps in the kitchen and the clink of washing dishes. Finally, the house grew silent. Had they forgotten him? Then, at long last, the wood box was moved and the panel opened.

chapter nine

Mama Petroski

The room was dark except for one small candle. Simon climbed out, stretching his cramped muscles. "We had to wait until people were asleep," Irena said softly. "I saved you some dinner."

"I need to use the bathroom," Simon said, embarrassed.

"Oh, my. Of course you do," she laughed. She led him to a tiny bathroom at the back of the house. When he returned to the kitchen, she had set a plate on the table, piled high with a good, thick stew of vegetables and meat.

"Eat quickly," she said. "Dominick will take you in a few minutes."

"I am very grateful," Simon said around bites of stew.

The woman shrugged. "It is not so much that we love Jews, as it is that we hate Germans."

Dominick came into the kitchen. "You don't walk with me. I will lead, you follow, but not so close that it looks like we are together. I will try to keep you out of danger, but if a patrol comes, you are on your own. Duck into an alley, or just run. The streetlights in this part of town were ruined in the bombing, so you should be able to get away. When you get where we are going, you forget me. Understood?"

Simon nodded solemnly.

"Let's go, then," Dominick said tersely. He stepped out of the door and, after a quick look around, started off at a brisk pace. Simon followed a short distance behind.

It was a dark, moonless night, and a cold wind blew between the darkened houses. They passed a few houses that had been reduced to rubble by German bombs. Simon shivered. The stew churned in his stomach. He glanced warily at each house as they passed. What if someone were to look out and see them?

Without warning, Dominick ducked into an alley. Simon quickly followed, and then strong hands grabbed him. "Get in the outhouse," Dominick hissed. At the same time, Simon heard the rumble of a truck coming slowly down the road.

A dilapidated outhouse was perched behind a house nearby in the alley. Simon slipped inside. He saw Dominick head for the rubble of a bombed-out house. Simon reached for the door but then changed his mind. The Germans might not search if the door was standing open. He flattened himself against the wall and listened

as the truck made its way down the street. Now he heard the sound of boots, and there was a flash of light across the outhouse door. Four soldiers walked up the alley, flashing their lights into garbage cans and wooden sheds. Suddenly, the light came on in the house and a voice called, "Who's there?"

The soldiers laughed. One of them said, "Go back to bed, old man. We are looking for escaped Jews."

"Good," the old man answered. "Catch one for me." Then he said, "I might as well relieve myself since I am up."

He opened the door and stepped in, pulling the door closed behind him. Simon's heart nearly stopped beating and he trembled in terror. The man held a lantern in one hand. He put his finger to his lips.

"Any Jews in there, old man?" called one of the soldiers with a laugh.

"Six or seven," the old man laughed. "Don't worry. I'll stuff them down the hole."

Laughing, the soldiers moved out of the alley, and Simon heard the truck moving down the road.

"I knew someone was in here when I saw the door open," the old man whispered.

"Thank you," Simon said simply.

"We've heard the fighting all day. It's not right, making war on women and children," the old man said. He held up the lantern. "You are only a child yourself. Is there anyone helping you?"

Simon nodded. "If I haven't lost him."

The old man shivered in his long, white nightshirt. "I'll go back in the house. Maybe he will come back for you."

Simon walked slowly up the alley toward the rubble where he had last seen Dominick. After a few panic-filled minutes, he found him, picking his way over broken walls and bricks. "You escaped," Dominick whispered. "Good."

He set off once more at a rapid pace. Simon dropped back as he had been instructed to and followed. They wound through a narrow, crooked alley behind a street of shops. Dominick tapped softly at a small door at the back of one of the shops. It was opened immediately.

"Good luck," Dominick said quietly. He set off back down the alley before Simon could thank him. The woman at the door was very short and extremely fat, but her face was kind. She wore a greasy apron over her clothes and her hair was pulled back tightly. They were in what looked to be a small restaurant, with tables and chairs scattered around the room. The tables were covered with brightly colored tablecloths, giving it a friendly atmosphere. Along one wall were open cupboards, and tiny glass figurines filled the shelves.

"I am Mrs. Petroski, and this is my restaurant," she said. "It's called Mama Petroski. The best food in all of Warsaw.

The Germans love it. They come to eat every day." Seeing his alarm, she chuckled so that her stomach rippled.

"Sometimes the best place to hide something is right under your nose." She pointed to one of the cupboards. "Wiggle that out from the wall. Be careful. Don't knock over any of my figurines." Simon took one side and pulled carefully. The cupboard moved easily away from the wall to reveal a narrow set of rickety steps leading down.

"It's an old cellar," she said. "When the restaurant was remodeled, we closed it up. Now no one even remembers it was there."

Simon looked down at the darkness, dreading it, but Mrs. Petroski handed him a candlestick. "There are no windows, so this will give you some light. You must be very quiet when the restaurant is open, though. I will try to find a better place as soon as I can."

Taking the candle, Simon headed down the stairs. The cellar was little more than a small room with a dirt floor. It had a damp, earthy smell. On one side were several small cots. A table and two chairs filled another corner. But the biggest surprise was that there were other people. At least a dozen people were squeezed into the tiny space.

The people in the cellar crowded around, peppering him with questions. What news did he have about the war? What was happening in the ghetto? At last, a man's voice rose above the rest. "Can't you see the boy is exhausted? There is time enough for all this later." One of the women pointed to a cot. "Sleep," she said. "We can talk tomorrow."

Simon lay down on the cot and closed his eyes. He was exhausted, but sleep eluded him. Was this going to be the rest of his life? Hiding in damp, dark cellars with strangers? The smell of so many unwashed bodies was overpowering. He thought about Jozef, his mother, his father, and little Anya. Were they still alive? And if they were, would he ever find them? He was weighed down with despair, and he wondered if it was even worth the fight to stay living. He breathed a shuddery sigh.

A soft hand stroked his shoulder. Startled, Simon opened his eyes and leaped up. "Ahh, child, don't be alarmed. I only wanted to give a bit of comfort." The woman leaning over the cot was old. Her face was lined with deep wrinkles, but it was still possible to see the great beauty she had once been. "If this place brings an old lady to despair, I can only imagine what it must be like for one so young. Children should be running and playing in the sunshine, but there are so few children left, and all of them are hiding in dark holes."

"I don't want to live in a world that could do this," Simon whispered, fighting back tears.

Anger flashed in her old blue eyes. "You must not think that way. You must be strong. You must live to tell the world what has happened to our people. And somehow you must use your anger to survive and then put it away so that you can live a full life."

Simon sighed without answering. "Not everyone is bad. Mrs. Petroski risks her life for us every day. She is not the only one. All over the country, I believe, there are Jews being hidden by good people," the woman said.

She moved away and Simon closed his eyes again. When he awoke it took him a minute to remember where he was.

Several people in the room made a motion for silence, pointing up. Simon could hear the sound of walking and the occasional chair scraping across the floor. Across the room he saw the woman from last night. She was sitting on one of the chairs, knitting. She looked up and smiled. Simon managed a weak smile back.

One by one, the people introduced themselves. The lady who had spoken to Simon was Mrs. Pryla. She thought that she was the only one left of her large family. They had lived in a small town near Warsaw, and the Germans had surrounded the town and killed or taken away all the Jews, including her husband, children, and grand-children. She had only survived because she was visiting a Christian friend.

"I lived next door to Mrs. Petroski when we were children," she told Simon. "We had remained friends, and when

Mrs. Petroski remembered the closed-off cellar, she brought me to Warsaw and hid me. That was two years ago."

Simon was horrified. "You have been here two years? How could you stand it?"

"It is not so bad," she replied. "At least I am alive."

As soon as Simon stood up, a man named Dudowski and his wife took his place. The man glared at Simon. "Next time, you take your turn like everyone else," he grumbled as he stretched out on the cot.

His wife gave Simon an apologetic smile. "He didn't know, Henryk," she said quietly.

Henryk merely grunted and rolled over.

"We take turns," one of the women explained. "There are only three cots. Each person gets four hours. It is the same with the chairs. You can sit at the table and play cards or just sit. The rest of the time we sit on the floor or walk about." She showed him where two buckets were for relieving himself. A blanket was hung on a rope for privacy.

"At night, when the restaurant is closed, we carry the buckets up and empty them. Mrs. Petroski makes us a meal," Mrs. Pryla told him. She gave Simon a small chunk of bread. "Tonight, save some of your bread for breakfast."

The day dragged on. Above them, Simon heard the sounds of the customers, the click of women's shoes, and occasionally the heavy tread of Nazi boots. At last, the restaurant grew quiet, and the cupboard slid open. Mrs. Petroski was there with a huge pot of vegetable soup, bread, and cheese. Minding what Mrs. Pryla had told him, Simon carefully saved some of the bread for the next day.

"I am looking for another hiding place for you," Mrs. Petroski said, patting Simon's shoulder. "You are fortunate, because you look like a Pole. We may have to change your name, and you will have to pretend you are a Christian, but it will be better than staying in a basement until the war ends."

"Thank you," Simon replied.

"Be patient. It may take some time," she said, patting him again.

All too soon, the cupboard was pushed back into place. Mrs. Petroski lived above the restaurant, and she was up late every night feeding the people in hiding. The women helped clean up the kitchen, so as not to have any evidence of Mrs. Petroski's nightly activities. Then their benefactor went to bed for a few hours of needed rest.

Days went by, and then weeks. Occasionally, Mrs. Petroski brought Simon a book to read, and once she gave them a thousand-piece puzzle that they set up on the table and took turns working on. Most of the time, however, they sat in silence, waiting for the evening meal.

Mrs. Pryla had been friendly with several Christian women before the war. She taught Simon what she could of the religion. "You will have to pretend to be Christian to survive," she said. "Never let anyone know you are a Jew. If they are suspicious, they may ask you questions about Christianity."

"The Christians have two main holidays: Christmas and Easter," she explained. "Christmas is when Jesus was born. They believe that after he was crucified, he rose from the dead on Easter."

"If he rose from the dead, why do they still hate us?" Simon asked. "And anyway, wasn't he a Jew?"

Mrs. Pryla chuckled. "And all of his disciples. But they seem to forget that." She was thoughtful for a time. "Of course, with Hitler and the Nazis it is even more than religion. They also make it about politics and race. Hitler blamed the problems in Germany after World War I on the Jews. He believes we are an inferior race, and it seems he's doing his best to get rid of us."

Mrs. Pryla also showed Simon how to make the sign of the cross and how to say a blessing before eating, making him repeat it until she was sure he would remember.

At last, one day, Mrs. Petroski said she had found a place for Simon. "A friend who lives in the country. The Germans don't come around much. We are going to say that you are a nephew and your parents were killed in the bombings. She really did lose her sister's family. She is

going to send for her real nephew's baptismal papers. Now all I have to do is figure out how to get you there."

A few weeks later, Mrs. Petroski told him he would be leaving in the morning.

"Your new name will be Feliks Moski," Mrs. Petroski informed him. "In the morning they clean up the streets and muck out the barns. They take it out to the country in a wagon and spread it on the fields. You will have to travel on the wagon. It will not be pleasant, but you should be safe. The driver will put fresh hay near his seat. You will hide yourself under the hay until you are out of town."

Simon was too tense to sleep. Before first light, Mrs. Petroski came for him. Mrs. Pryla gave him a warm sweater she had knit for him. She wiped tears from her eyes as she hugged him.

"I will never forget you," Simon whispered.

Mrs. Petroski handed him a small backpack. "There is a clean shirt and pants inside," she said.

Simon rolled up the sweater from Mrs. Pryla and tucked it into the pack. They waited together until the wagon came rumbling down the alley. Mrs. Petroski looked about carefully. "Thank you for everything," Simon whispered.

"Go," she said, shoving him gently out the door. "God watch over you."

The hay wagon barely slowed down as Simon ran out and jumped into it. He buried himself under the clean hay and burrowed up against the back of the driver's seat. As Mrs. Petroski had warned, the smell was terrible, and he suspected his shoes and pants were soiled.

The horse maintained a steady pace. Suddenly, Simon heard the driver swear. "German patrol, boy. Don't make a sound."

The soldiers demanded the driver's papers. While they were being inspected, one of the soldiers came to the back of the wagon. Taking the pitchfork, he stabbed several times through the muck. Simon felt a burning pain in his thigh, but he bit his lip to keep from crying out or moving. At last, the patrol left, and the driver started on his way again.

"Are you all right?" the driver asked softly after a few minutes.

"I think so," Simon replied, "but my leg is bleeding."

The horse plodded on. It was a breathtakingly hot day, and the terrible smell and loss of blood were making Simon sick to his stomach.

"Can we stop for a minute?" Simon pleaded desperately. "I think I am going to be sick."

The driver swore again, but he stopped the wagon. "Be quick about it," he growled.

Simon climbed painfully out of the wagon. They were next to a large cornfield. The stalks were almost as tall as Simon and just starting to tassel. A ditch ran along the side of the road. He leaned into the ditch and vomited. He could see that his wound was worse than he had thought. His pants were ripped and a deep gash ran across his thigh. Blood had soaked through his pants, making the cloth stick to his leg.

Suddenly, the driver hissed, "There is a German truck heading toward us. Run into the cornfield and hide before they see you."

Simon ran into the rows of corn. His wound made him limp, but he tried to disregard the pain and move deeper into the rows of tall corn. Afraid that the Germans would see the stalks moving, he lay flat between the rows, hoping he was far enough in that he wouldn't be seen. His heart was pounding, and he felt dizzy from the pain. If the soldiers came into the cornfield, he was not sure he could escape. After a time, he heard the truck move on. He lay still for a few more minutes then cautiously worked his way back to the road. The sun beat down on the pavement, sending shimmers of heat waves in the air. There was no sign of the German truck. There was also no sign of the wagon.

chapter ten

A New Home

Summer 1943

Simon perched on the edge of the ditch, waiting for the driver to return. After the shock of not seeing the wagon, he had managed to calm down. No doubt the German soldiers watched the wagon drive away. The driver would wait a respectable amount of time and return when he was certain the Germans were gone.

It was hot waiting. Insects buzzed around his wounded leg, and he brushed them away. Each time, they flew up in a cloud of tiny wings only to land again, drawn by the blood-soaked pants. After a while, he quit trying to brush them off.

The hours dragged by. There was little traffic on the road. Twice a German truck passed, forcing Simon to dive back into the cornfield. There was an occasional car and two or three wagons, but none of them were the hay wagon returning for him. He waited for several hours before he

decided that the driver was not coming back. Perhaps the driver had been too spooked by the second encounter with soldiers, or maybe they had followed him. Whatever the reason, it was plain that he had been abandoned. Even worse, he had left his pack on the wagon.

His leg was getting stiff, and it felt hot to the touch, but at least the bleeding had stopped. He remembered that his mother had always washed cuts, worried about infection. He thought about the dirty pitchfork. He needed to find someplace to clean his wound. Reluctantly, with one last look down the empty road, he walked back into the cornfield. His leg hurt terribly as he trudged slowly through the rows. The stalks scratched his skin and made him itch, but he scarcely noticed. He had no idea what to do now. Mrs. Petroski had not told him the would-be benefactor's name or even where she lived.

Through everything so far, he had never been utterly alone. He realized that he had no one to depend on except for himself. As he stumbled through the cornfield, he tried to think of a way to survive. He would use the name Mrs. Petroski had given him. If his benefactor lived nearby, perhaps she would hear of him and come to his aid.

He looked up at the sky. It was late afternoon, and he would have to find a place to sleep soon. His throat was parched and he needed water.

He was nearly out of the cornfield when he heard voices. He crouched down and cautiously peeked out from behind the stalks. The next field was planted with a different crop. He had never been around a farm before. He wasn't sure what it was. Two men were hoeing between the rows. They laughed and joked with each other as they worked. His instincts told him to stay hidden. He remained crouched, watching as the men worked, hoeing row after row. At last, one of them pulled out a pocket watch and checked it. Putting their hoes over their shoulders, they walked toward a small line of trees and disappeared.

After he was sure the men would not return, Simon stepped out of the cornfield and inspected the plants. They still did not look familiar. He pulled one out of the ground. To his delight there were small brown bulbs attached to the roots. Potatoes! He brushed off the dirt and bit into one. He broke off the rest and stuffed his pockets. Then he threw the plant into the cornfield to hide it. He followed the same path the men had taken. Now he could see that a narrow, rough gravel road divided the cornfield. The trees lined a small creek. A wooden bridge had been built across it, wide enough for a wagon, and beyond that the road continued, dusty and silent.

Simon climbed down the bank of the stream. The water was slightly muddy, but it was cool. He cupped his hands and drank. Then he took off his pants and washed his wound the best that he could. He ripped off the bottom of his shirt and tied it around his leg. Then he dipped his pants several times in the water. The stream turned red, washing away his blood. It was so hot he knew his pants would dry quickly. He hung them on a board under the bridge, hoping no one would come. It was almost dark now, so he gathered up grass from alongside the road and piled it where he thought he would be hidden if anyone drove across the bridge. He sat down and ate the rest of the potatoes, wishing he had some way to cook them. At last, he curled up on his grass bed and fell asleep.

The sun woke him early the next morning, and he discovered that mosquitoes had feasted on him during the night. He unwrapped his leg and stared at it. It was swollen, red, and starting to fester. He reached for his pants and pulled them on just as a wagon and horses headed over the bridge. He stayed still while it rumbled over his head and continued down the road. When he judged that it was out of sight, he hobbled out and climbed up the bank. He crossed the bridge and walked painfully in the opposite direction. He saw trees in the distance and headed toward them. When he reached the forest, he sat on a fallen log to think about what to do next. It was cooler here, at least. A small breeze blew through the green leaves.

It was not a large forest, but it was big enough to hide him, he thought. The only sounds were the buzzing of insects and the chirps of birds flitting among the trees. He walked deeper into the woods and found some small berry bushes. The berries were sour and not quite ripe, but he ate them anyway.

He stayed in the forest for three days. Each time the farm workers went home, he came out of his hiding spot and painfully walked across the bridge. With a stick he dug around a potato plant, carefully removing a potato and patting the earth down around it so it would not be noticed. At night, he wiggled into a hollow log and slept.

One day, he slowly and painfully climbed a tree. His leg was throbbing, and he had to cling to the trunk while a wave of dizziness swept over him. When his head cleared, he looked in every direction. He was not far from a village. He could see a dozen houses and a small church. There were several houses on the road leading to town. The tree was a large one, with a comfortable crook about halfway up. He sat in the tree most of the day, watching the nearby houses.

Suddenly, he heard twigs cracking like someone was walking in the woods. He had been sitting in the crook with his legs dangling down on either side. He stood up and hugged the trunk. A minute later a man walked by the tree. The man had a rifle slung over one shoulder, and Simon thought he was looking for something. He even bent down and looked in the hollow log that Simon had slept in, but

he did not look up. After a while, the man left the forest and walked down the road toward the village. Had someone seen him? Simon stayed in the tree until it was almost dark.

The next morning, his leg was still red and festering, even though he had washed it each day in the stream. He walked down the road to the nearest house. He had seen a woman there, but no man. He crouched in some tall grass and watched.

A woman came out of the house and started hanging clothes on a line. A large brown dog barked as Simon approached and, startled, the woman looked up from her basket and stared at him.

"Please," Simon said. "Could you give me something to eat and maybe some salve for my leg?"

"What is your name?" she asked.

"Feliks Moski," Simon answered.

"You are not from around here," she said, still staring at him.

"I am an orphan," Simon answered. "My parents were killed in the bombing."

The woman was middle-aged and thin, with blue eyes and a big smile. "Come with me," she said, leading him into the house. The kitchen was small. There was a wood stove, an iron sink with a pump, and a small table with two chairs. She cut him a piece of bread and buttered it, then poured him a glass of milk. Simon wolfed it down.

The woman studied him while he ate. "What happened to your leg?"

"I cut it on a fence," Simon said.

"Take off your pants so I can treat it," the woman said.

Simon blushed. "I don't have any underwear."

The woman laughed. It was a friendly, throaty laugh, and Simon smiled back, although he was still very embarrassed. She went into another room and returned with a large pair of undershorts. "I will turn my back. Put these on. They are too big, but they will cover you."

Simon took off his pants and put on the shorts. He sat back down on the chair. "Do these belong to your husband?" he asked.

The woman sighed. "He is dead."

She looked at the leg, making clucking noises. "This is bad. I think I can help it, but it may hurt."

Simon shrugged. "It does already."

The woman took a knife and scraped open the scabs. Then she took a strong, harsh soap and scrubbed the wound, rinsing several times. Simon bit his lip to keep from crying out. The woman put on a smelly black salve, and then she cut a clean cloth into strips and wrapped it around his leg. She handed him back his pants and he pulled them on.

"How old are you?" she asked.

"Thirteen," Simon answered. "Nearly fourteen."

"You are small for your age. Well, Feliks, would you like to stay here? My name is Mrs. Cecylia Jaworska. My husband died last year, and I could use some help."

Simon could not believe his good fortune. "Yes," he said, nodding. He followed her outside. A small, neat garden was planted along the side of the house and there were two pear trees. There were several small buildings. One was a sheep shed, and a larger barn housed two cows. Half a dozen chickens pecked for bugs near the barn.

There was a well, and Mrs. Jaworska showed him how to crank up the bucket and bring water to the sheep and cows. She showed him a large burlap bag of grain, and he sprinkled some for the chickens. Then she took out a stool and started to milk the cows while he watched. Simon had never been around large farm animals. He found the cows a little frightening. But Mrs. Jaworska patted them and spoke to them as she milked.

"I make cheese with the milk," she explained. "I sell the cheese and wool from the sheep and a few eggs in the village."

"Your job will be to take the sheep and cows to the pasture and make sure they do not get into the neighbors' beet field. At night you can help hoe the garden."

Mrs. Jaworska made supper for the two of them. It was noodles with a cream sauce and an omelet. Simon picked up his fork to eat, but Mrs. Jaworska gave him a look. She crossed herself. Simon did the same and, remembering what Mrs. Pryla had taught him, he said, "Bless us our Lord and these thy gifts, which we are about to receive."

Mrs. Jaworska smiled when he said the blessing. When they finished their meal, she handed him a long white nightshirt. "Put this on. I will wash your clothes." She gave him an old blanket. "You can sleep in the sheep shed. Make yourself a bed in the hay."

Simon took the blanket and spread it across the sweet-smelling hay. He thought about Mrs. Jaworska. He had not found the woman who would get him papers, but maybe he would be safe here. In only a few minutes, he fell sound asleep.

The next morning, when he returned to the house, Mrs. Jaworska had a large tub in the kitchen, filled with hot water. "I had to burn your clothes," she said. "They were crawling with lice."

She handed him the strong-smelling soap she had used on his leg. "Scrub yourself good." She unwrapped his leg and examined it. "It looks better, but scrub it again, too."

Simon sank into the hot water. It was the first bath he had taken since the day his mother and Anya had been taken away. When he climbed out, the water was gray. He wrapped up in the large towel she had left for him and called, "I am done."

Mrs. Jaworska came back to the kitchen. She made him sit down. Then she shaved his head. She took a cloth and rubbed his head with kerosene. It burned his eyes and scalp, but she made him wait several minutes before she washed it off. When she was satisfied, she handed him a pair of pants and a shirt. They fit perfectly.

"I cut down some of my husband's clothes last night to fit you," she said.

She led him to the barn. A path ran along behind it. Mrs. Jaworska whistled and started walking along the path. To Simon's great surprise, the cows followed, and the sheep trailed after them. She handed him some bread and cheese wrapped in newspaper. "All you have to do is watch them. Don't let them get in the neighbors' fields."

Simon felt a moment of panic. The cows were very big. "How do I stop them?"

Mrs. Jaworska laughed her infectious laugh again. "Just wave your arms and steer them back. You are the boss." She walked back down the path and disappeared.

Simon watched the cows and sheep carefully. But they seemed content enough in the meadow. After a few minutes, he sat on a rock. He wished he had a book to read. He decided he would ask her if she had any that evening.

After a time one of the cows wandered near the wheat. Simon panicked, but the cow ambled away when he raised his arms and shouted. When he judged it was noon, he unwrapped his lunch and ate every crumb.

Late in the afternoon, he began to worry about getting the cows home. He whistled as Mrs. Jaworska had done, and, to his amazement, the cows looked up from their eating and followed him down the path.

Mrs. Jaworska smiled at him that evening. "Did you have any trouble?" she asked.

Simon shook his head. "No," he said proudly. "I think they like me."

The woman nodded. She fed him a supper of thick stew with vegetables. After dinner he helped her with the dishes. "You are a good boy," Mrs. Jaworska said. "Did you help your mother like this?"

Simon shook his head. "No, but I wish that I had." A wave of sadness washed over him as he thought of his brave mother. He wiped at his eyes.

Mrs. Jaworska noticed. "I did not mean to bring back painful memories. When people are taken from us, there are always regrets. I'm sure your mother was very proud of you."

After the dishes were done, she took him to the garden and showed him how to hoe the weeds without damaging the vegetables. Simon's hands soon became sor. He saw that he was getting a blister. "I can see that you were definitely a city boy," Mrs. Jaworska said when she saw it.

When they finished, she put some of the black salve on his sore hands.

The next morning, Simon asked her if she had any books. "I can't read," she admitted. "I might be able to find you one in the village. I will ask on Sunday when I go to church." She hesitated, and Simon thought she would invite him to go with her, but she did not. Her silence made Simon wonder if she suspected he was a Jew.

Every morning Simon took the cows and the sheep to the pasture. It was lonely, but he looked forward to the evenings. Mrs. Jaworska told him about how her husband had been killed when he was cutting a tree for firewood and it fell on him.

"We had six cows and twenty sheep," she said. "But the Nazis confiscated some of them. It seems as though Hitler's army can't run without stealing from a widow." She sighed. "At least they left me the ones I have. I should not complain. They are doing much worse to the Jews." She gave him a sharp look. "You probably don't know much about the war outside Poland."

When Simon shook his head, the woman said, "The Russians are beating back the Germans, and both England and America have bombed Germany. The end is in sight. But it is too late for those people left in the Warsaw ghetto. They fought them off for weeks, but in the end, the Nazis reduced the ghetto to rubble."

A New Home

Simon stumbled away, too overcome with grief to speak. He slept fitfully that night.

*****

On Sunday, Mrs. Jaworska put on her hat and walked to the village to church. When she returned she had a book. It was a book of fairy tales, too young for Simon, but he thanked her. "Would you read it to me?" she asked.

After dinner, they sat at the table instead of hoeing, and Simon read. Mrs. Jaworska seemed entranced. "My father did not think girls needed to go to school," she said.

"Maybe I could teach you," Simon offered.

Her eyes lit up. "Do you think I could really learn?" she asked.

He showed her some letters. "All the letters have sounds," he said. "When you learn all the sounds, you can put them together to make words."

The weeks went by. It was autumn and the nights were getting colder. Simon and Mrs. Jaworska harvested the remaining vegetables from the garden and stored them in a root cellar. After dinner, Mrs. Jaworska brewed them a cup of tea, and they worked on her lesson. Afterward, Simon would read while she listened in rapt attention. Sometimes they listened to her radio, trying to follow the war. The Americans had taken back Italy, and, in October, they heard that Italy had joined the war against the Germans.

"Why don't they come here to help us?" Simon cried in frustration.

Sometimes people came to Mrs. Jaworska's house to buy cheese or fresh eggs. Simon always hid in the barn when people came. If Mrs. Jaworska noticed, she didn't comment.

One day, when Mrs. Jaworska came home from church, she looked worried. "I think I have done something terrible. People teased me about my sudden interest in books. I told them that I had an orphan living here, and someone must have told the forester. He takes care of the forest, but he also acts as our police constable. Today, he started asking me questions about you. I told him what you said, that your parents were killed in the bombing. He said people had noticed you do not go to church."

"My parents were not religious," Simon said.

"I told him that, but he wants to see your papers."

"I don't have any," Simon said. "They were lost."

"What is the name of the town you lived in? The forester could get copies."

"I don't remember," Simon said.

Mrs. Jaworska sighed. "Are you a Jew?"

Stricken with dread, Simon nodded.

"You must go quickly. He is coming in a few minutes to see you." She gave him a pack and he stuffed in his clothes. She wrapped up a loaf of bread and a large wedge of cheese.

"Don't go into the forest. He is sure to look there. Go past the village. He won't be expecting that. About thirty miles more and there is a very large forest. Perhaps you can hide there."

"Will you be in trouble?" Simon asked.

She shrugged. "I came home and mentioned the forester was coming to visit, and you ran away." She gave him a quick hug. "Go quickly." She kissed his cheek. "May your God protect you."

chapter eleven

On the Run

Simon ran behind the barn and through the neighbors' fields. He saw the forester's car driving on the road, heading for Mrs. Jaworska's house, and he crouched low, hoping he had not seen him. He ran most of the day, trying to get as much distance as he could from Mrs. Jaworska's house. He passed the village, staying away from the road and cutting through fields of corn and potatoes. When night came, Simon found a large haystack in a field and burrowed into it to hide.

He thought he would find the forest in three days or possibly four, but by the fifth day he decided he had missed it somehow. Simon had heard that sometimes people can get lost and walk in a circle, ending up back where they started. He passed another village and was relieved that it was not the one by Mrs. Jaworska's house. This village was built on the banks of a river. Simon looked at the river in dismay. It was wide and muddy brown, so he could not tell how deep it was. At any rate, it was much too cold. Simon walked along the bank, trying to find a place to cross. There was a road and a bridge in the village, but he would have to go into the village to reach it.

Simon crouched in the tall grass and watched the bridge. There was a surprising amount of traffic. He watched men riding bicycles and farm wagons, an occasional car, and more disturbing, German motorcycles. Once, a German truck loaded with many soldiers passed over the bridge. Obviously, this was a main thoroughfare. As he observed, Simon ate the last of the bread and cheese Mrs. Jaworska had given him.

Following the river, Simon walked away from the town, trying to look like any local boy. As he walked, he found a straight stick and picked it up. He laid it across his shoulders, hoping that from a distance it would look like a fishing pole.

Suddenly, a large black-and-white dog burst out of the tall grass, barking and showing his teeth. "Hold him, King," a voice shouted. Two older boys came out of the grass at the edge of the river. The dog snapped his teeth at Simon. Almost without thinking, he took the stick and struck it sharply across the dog's nose, shouting "No!" at the same time. The dog yelped and slunk away.

"You hit my dog," said one of the boys, with an angry scowl. He balled his hands into fists.

"You told him to bite me," Simon protested.

"I only told him to watch you," the boy said. "Who are you, anyway? You don't come from around here."

"I am looking for work," Simon said. "I am an orphan. My parents were killed in the bombings."

Simon still gripped the stick. The boys circled him warily. "You're a Jew," the other boy said.

"No, I'm not," Simon said.

"I'll bet you are one of them hiding in the forest."

"What forest?" Simon asked.

The boy with the dog waved his arm carelessly across the river.

"I am on this side of the river," Simon said reasonably.

"Go get the Gestapo," the first boy said suddenly. "I'll watch him. We might get a reward if he is a Jew."

Simon's stomach lurched in fear as he remembered Lydia's story of how the Gestapo tortured people. He watched the second boy as he ran off toward the town, trying to come up with a plan for escape. The boy with the dog watched Simon. His dog stood beside him. Simon inched his way so that he was standing on the riverbank.

Suddenly, he jumped into the dark water. He heard the boy shouting, but he struck out for the opposite shore. The water was freezing. Simon swam furiously, but his body was growing numb. Then, just as he thought he would die there in the muddy water, his foot hit the bottom and he pulled himself up on the other shore. He was aware of shouting. The boy had returned with the Gestapo. Simon scrambled to his feet and ran. He heard the crack of gunfire, and a bullet whizzed by his head as he raced desperately away.

Simon's body shook violently. He knew it was only a matter of minutes before the Gestapo crossed the bridge and came after him. He looked for a place to hide. Far ahead he saw a cornfield. Shaking so much he could hardly run, he tumbled toward it. By the time he reached it, he could hear shouting some distance behind him. He plunged into the tall stalks.

A small stream divided the cornfield. The stream led back to the river and a small cluster of trees and bushes. He ducked down into the gully made by the stream and ran back to the river. He was sure the men had seen him head into the cornfield. If he was lucky, they would not search along the riverbank, thinking he would be running away from it. He reached the brush and lay down flat, pulling brush over himself. He heard shouting in the cornfield and the splashing of boots as his pursuers crossed the stream. There was a loud crack of rifle fire and a scream. Someone else must have been hiding in the cornfield. He heard more shots, but he lay down without moving for what seemed to be forever. At last, he heard the men returning. They were

laughing and talking in German. One of them walked only a few yards away from Simon's hiding place.

Simon waited until almost dark before he dared move. His body felt numb, although he was still shivering violently. He was so exhausted that he had to fight the urge to just curl up and sleep. He slowly made his way back along the stream to the cornfield. There was enough moonlight that he could see a little as he staggered through the rows. He had to find some sort of shelter, some way to dry his clothes. His pack that held his extra clothes had fallen off in the river.

He stumbled over something soft. It took him a second to realize it was a body. The man was lying between two rows of corn, his face frozen in a mask of pain. Simon moaned, staring at the man. Had he caused this man's death by running into the cornfield? He thought about the man's clothes. They were ragged, but dry. He had seen a lot of dead bodies since the day of the bombing so long ago. Still, in the end, he could not make himself undress the man. He checked in the pockets of his coat, hoping to find food. There was a box of matches in one pocket. In the other was a slingshot. He put them in his own pockets and walked on.

A brisk, icy wind had come up. It dried Simon's clothes a little but chilled him even more. He came at last to a huge manor house. The house had a circular driveway and a new car was parked in front. Beyond the house were several barns and a cottage, possibly for a caretaker. All the windows were dark and silent. He slipped behind the house and ran to the first barn. It was latched with a bar. If he took shelter in there, they would know someone was there. The second building, a sheep shed, had hay stored at one end. Simon climbed into the hay, burrowing underneath for warmth. In a minute, he was fast asleep.

Simon only slept for a few hours. When he woke, he felt feverish and weak with hunger. He saw smoke rising from the chimney on the caretaker's cottage. He staggered to the door and knocked.

The old woman who answered the door stared at him. "Please," Simon said. "Could you give me something to eat?"

The woman hesitated. From another room, a man's voice called, "Who is there?"

"It's a boy," said the woman. "He is asking for food."

The man walked into the kitchen. He was tall and thin, and his face was leathery, as if he had spent most of his years outdoors. "Please," Simon mumbled.

"I wish we could hide you, but it is not possible," the man said. "All these lands belong to Mr. Walczak. He has been away on business but will return tomorrow. We think he is a collaborator with the Nazis. German high officials often come to his house for dinner."

"There is a very big forest not too far from here," the woman said.

"I will take you," the man said. "There are others hiding there. Maybe they can help you."

The woman made Simon a good breakfast. She gave him aspirin for his fever and rubbed a warm salve on his chest. Then she packed a knapsack with a blanket, extra socks, several tins of food, a large cheese, and some bread. She tucked in his matches and slingshot, a small knife, and a large piece of oiled cloth.

"This may keep you dry when it rains," she said. She gave him one of the man's old coats, which was too big but warm.

The man saddled one of the horses and helped Simon get on. Simon had never been on a horse, and he clung on tightly as they rode through the field toward the dark line of trees in the distance. When they arrived, he slid off the horse and watched as the man rode away.

Simon walked deeper into the forest, looking for a place to hide. After an hour of hiking, he found a narrow ravine with thick undergrowth. He crawled underneath the thickest part and pushed the branches apart so that he had a space large enough to sit or lie down. He spread the blanket and sat on it while he ate some of the bread and cheese.

Leaving his pack hidden, the next morning he set off to explore. He found a few dried berries left on the bushes, but nothing else that looked edible. He set up a piece of wood on a stump, and he took out the slingshot and practiced. At first, his aim was wildly off, but finally he was able to knock the wood off the stump.

The next day it rained. It was a cold, miserable rain that lasted most of the day. Simon took off the coat and used it like a blanket. Then he stretched the oilcloth over himself and managed to stay mostly dry and warm. He had planned to try his hand at hunting, but everything was too wet to start a fire, so he ate some more of the cheese and the last of the bread. There was a good moon that night, so he walked out of the forest and dug some potatoes from a nearby field. There was a stream, but he had nothing to carry water. He cupped the water in his hands and drank.

Not far from the stream was a house. He could see the glow of light from the window. Cautiously looking for dogs, he made his way to the house and peeked in the window. There was a family eating dinner. The woman was laughing at something and the children smiled, too. There were two boys just a little younger than him, and a girl about Anya's age. It looked like his family a few years ago. He watched them for a long time, sorrow and loneliness washing over him so that he could hardly move. At last, he walked to a small shed. There was a shovel leaning against the door, and inside the door he found a bucket. Gripping his new treasures, he ran back to his camp.

The next day he killed a rabbit with his slingshot. It was more luck than skill. The hapless rabbit hopped into the clearing just as Simon was preparing to practice again. Seeing Simon, it froze, giving Simon just enough time to aim. His father had given him a book about outdoor skills when he was younger. He knew he had to remove the guts of the rabbit. Taking a breath, he sliced into the rabbit with his knife. To his surprise, it was steamy hot inside. Gagging a little, he reached in and cleaned out the insides. Then he cut off the head and feet. Taking the shovel, he buried them with the entrails. Then he carefully cut off the skin, setting it aside. He waited until night time to cook the rabbit. He dug a small hole some distance from his camp and made the fire inside, where it would not show. Then he found two forked branches and made a spit to cook the rabbit. After he finished eating, he buried the bones and the evidence of his fire. Feeling full and rather satisfied, he crawled into his hiding place and fell asleep.

Simon was aware that there were other people hiding in the forest. He occasionally smelled campfires or heard the crackle of someone passing through the brush, but he seldom saw anyone. He was so lonely that he often thought about going to one of the farms and asking for work. Winter was coming and he wasn't sure he could survive alone. He took his bucket with him each night, filling it with potatoes, beets, and carrots. With the shovel he dug a large hole, lining it with grasses and burying the vegetables for later. He moved from field to field, trying not to take so much that farmers would get suspicious. Always he paused to gaze in the windows of the nearby farmhouses. As the weeks went by, his loneliness grew, making him ache, and he woke up at night crying.

One day, three men with rifles slung across their shoulders passed silently not far from his camp. Simon hid behind a tree, not daring to breathe. Should he reveal himself? Perhaps they would talk to him if nothing else. They might be partisans, but he could not be sure. Even if they were, he had heard that some of them hated Jews, too. He remained motionless, agonizing over his decision until it was too late, and they had disappeared down the trail. Another day a man rode down a trail on a horse. Simon thought he must be the forester. He hid behind some trees and, after that, avoided going near any of the trails that cut through the woods. He was getting to be a sure shot with his slingshot, hitting his target more often than not. Even so, he was hungry all the time.

Finally, one day he decided he could stand it no longer. He carefully hid all his belongings and walked to a farmhouse. He did not go to the one with the children. He had watched them doing chores and reasoned they would be less likely to need help. The next farm looked fairly prosperous, with a large herd of cows and several pigs.

He knew there were a man and woman there, and they had a small baby. He walked to the door and knocked.

The man opened the door, eyeing him suspiciously.

"Do you have any food?" Simon asked. "I am willing to work for it."

"What can you do?" the man asked.

"I can herd your cows," Simon said. "Or chop your firewood," he added, noticing a large pile of heavy logs.

"Have you split logs before?" the man asked.

"No," Simon said honestly, "but I am strong. I am sure I can do it."

"You look too puny to be worth much," the man said with a snort. But he led Simon to the pile of logs and pointed to it. "Go to it."

The man leaned against the wall of a small shed, smirking when Simon picked up the large ax and swung it. The man took several large swallows from a flask. "You really are a dumb city boy," he said at last. He showed Simon how to split the wood using a wedge and a maul. He watched as Simon struggled with the first few logs but finally mastered it.

"Well, you learn fast enough," he said grudgingly. "You can sleep in the barn. My wife will give you supper."

Simon learned he was not to eat with the family. Every evening the wife scurried out to the barn with a plate of food, and every morning she gave him a piece of bread and some cheese, more if her husband was not around. The man often rode his motorcycle into town, coming back late at night staggering drunk. From the barn, Simon could hear shouting, and the next day the wife would have fresh bruises on her face and arms.

On most days, Simon was sent to watch the herd while it grazed in a distant pasture. The man had eight cows and they were not as tame as Mrs. Jaworska's had been. Simon was busy all day, trying to keep them out of neighboring fields. As soon as he would chase back one, another would be walking into another field. One day, three of the cows headed out of the pasture. Taking a stick and shouting, Simon managed to turn them away. Then he noticed that two others had gotten out on the other side of the pasture. Before he could reach them, the man suddenly appeared. He hit Simon several times, knocking him to the ground. "I'm not keeping you to let these cows get away," he shouted angrily.

Simon got up and hurried over to the two wayward cows. He was seething in anger, but he hid it. The man watched silently for a minute. Then he turned abruptly and headed back down the path. Simon stared after him, trying to decide if he should go back to the forest. But the woman's meals were good and, even though it was winter, the barn was warm enough with the blanket and straw.

One day, the man rode off to the village. It was warmer than usual and all of Simon's chores were finished. He knocked at the door.

"Could I take a bath?" he asked the man's wife.

She pointed to the large metal tub on the porch. "You can use that," she said. She fetched a cauldron and helped him make a fire to heat water from the well. She went back in the house and returned with a fine-tooth comb and a clean nightshirt. "You had better wash your clothes, too," she said.

Simon dragged the tub beside the barn, where it could not be seen from the house. When the water was warm, he filled several large buckets and scrubbed his clothes, wringing them out and laying them across a bush when he was done. He fetched more water from the well, and, while it heated, he combed his hair, knocking the lice into the fire. He combed until he could find no more, then, taking another bucket, he washed his hair. At last, the water was steaming hot. He dipped out bucketfuls, filling the tub, and each time replacing the water in the cauldron. Finally, he had enough for a bath. He stepped in and scrubbed himself.

The water was black with dirt and it was getting cold. Simon stood up to put on the nightshirt when suddenly the man appeared.

"You city boys can't take a little dirt?" he asked. Then he said, "You are a Jew."

Simon slipped on the shirt, but before he could speak, the man began beating him. "You have endangered my family, you dirty Jew," he said.

Picking up a board, he struck Simon, knocking him down and then viciously kicking him. Simon struggled, trying to stand up again, but the man hit him again and again until he was almost senseless. Then, dragging Simon by the arm, he threw him into a small shed and locked the door. A minute later, the motorcycle roared out of the yard.

"Are you all right?" the woman asked a few minutes later.

"Let me out, please," Simon muttered between bruised and swelling lips. There was a terrible pain in his side, and it was difficult to breathe.

"I can't," the woman wailed. "He would beat me if he comes back and sees that I have freed you."

"Please," Simon begged. "They will kill me."

The woman was silent for a few minutes. Then she said, "I have an idea. I will open the door and give you the wedge and maul. The wood is old. It should break. He will think you put the tools away in the shed and he didn't notice." She opened the door and handed the tools to Simon.

Simon took the maul, but when he tried to swing it, the pain in his side made him cry out. The woman picked up

the maul. "Hold the wedge," she said. Simon worked it into place in the crack between two boards. The woman swung the maul with every bit of her strength and there was a satisfying crack. She swung once more and the boards broke in half, leaving enough room to squeeze out. She locked the door and handed him his still-wet clothes.

"Wait," she said. She dashed back into the house and returned with a long strip of cloth. "Lift up your shirt," she ordered.

Simon winced in great pain when he did as she asked. "I think you have a broken rib," she said as she wrapped the strip tightly around him.

"Thank you," Simon whispered.

The woman nodded. "Run," she said. "They will be back soon."

Clutching his side, Simon ran. It was almost dark, for which he was grateful. His breath came in short, sharp bursts as he stumbled across the pastures and the neighbors' fields. Several times he stopped, willing himself to keep moving in spite of the agony. He could see the dark shadows of the forest ahead of him, but he was disoriented. He crouched down, resting for a moment, trying to remember the way he had taken when he first went to the farm. He crossed a potato field, recently harvested, and he stumbled over the newly turned earth. He thought he saw movement some distance away and wondered if another hidden person was gleaning the field, looking for small potatoes lost in the harvest.

Forcing himself to move, he staggered across the field and into the safety of the trees. He was a long way away from his old camp. He followed the forester's trail, just barely visible in the moonlight, stopping to rest every few feet. It was almost morning when he finally found his hiding place in the gully. He wiggled under the brambles and then froze. Before he had left he had carefully folded his blanket and oilcloth and stowed them in his backpack. Now he could see the oilcloth, spread out and, even more alarming, he could see the shape of a person underneath.

chapter twelve

Rutka

"This is my place," Simon whispered hoarsely. The numbing pain in Simon's side made it hard for him to even speak. He sank to the ground.

"You left it," said a familiar voice. "How was I to know you were coming back?"

"Rutka?" Simon whispered, hardly daring to believe it.

Rutka's curly mass of hair and her little, sharp face peered out from under the oilcloth. "Simon?" She sounded equally incredulous. She reached over and gave him a fierce bear hug, which made him yelp in pain.

With the first light of day filtering through the leafless trees, she examined his face. One of Simon's eyes was swollen completely shut and had turned dark purple. In addition, dried blood trickled from his nose, and his lip was cracked and swollen. "Oh, Simon," she moaned.

"I'll be all right if I can sleep," Simon said, crawling under the oilcloth in the warm spot Rutka had left.

"I'll get some water to clean you up," she said. Taking an old, dented pan, she slipped away. When she returned, Rutka tenderly washed the dried blood off Simon's face. Then she folded a bit of cool, wet cloth and put it on his eye. Before she was done, Simon had fallen asleep.

When he awoke it was late afternoon, and Rutka was sitting beside him, watching anxiously. "The forester passed by a few minutes ago," she whispered. "You have been moaning in your sleep, and I was afraid he would hear your voice."

"I'm sorry," Simon said. "I've put you in danger."

Rutka shrugged. "Lucky for both of us, you were silent."

"They told me you had been caught in a roundup," Simon said.

Rutka's smile was twisted. "I was. They took us all to the train station and started loading people into cattle cars. I heard one of the guards say 'Treblinka,' and I knew we were all going to die. Then I saw a drainpipe. So many people were crowded around that the guards didn't notice when I crawled inside. Lucky for me, I was skinny enough. The drain went into the sewers. I had to wade through filthy water and then wait under a manhole until it was dark. Then I just started walking."

"Didn't anyone help you?" Simon asked, thinking of the people who had helped him escape.

Rutka shrugged. "Mostly I stole food. Sometimes I begged. I stayed at one house for a few weeks. I helped with the housework and took care of the children. But her husband grabbed me one day. When I fought and kicked him, he said he knew I was a Jew, and he was going to turn me in. I ran away. When I got to the forest, I met an old farmer and his wife. They helped me."

Rutka cried when Simon told her about Jozef. Then she wiped her eyes with clenched fists. "I didn't think I had any tears left," she said.

"Maybe he will survive," Simon said. "Jozef doesn't look strong, but he is."

Rutka watched over Simon for three days. They talked a little, but mostly Simon slept. The bruises and cuts began to heal a little, although his rib was still painful when he moved. It was winter, but the weather had been mild. After four days, however, the weather turned bitterly cold and a freezing rain began to fall. Although they huddled together under the oilcloth, their bodies shook with cold.

"We can't go on like this," Rutka said. "The food is almost gone and there is nothing left in the fields." She crept out to retrieve a few potatoes she had hidden in a hollow tree. When she returned there was a middle-aged man and woman with her. "This is Moshe," she told Simon. "He and his wife, Sarah, are the ones who helped me. They have been hiding in the woods for two years."

Moshe squatted down. "When winter started we dug a shelter. Like this." He drew a rectangle in the dirt with a stick. "Like a grave. When we find a new place, we are thinking about one like this." He drew another rectangle crossing the first. "It is warmer under the ground, and it will be big enough for four."

"We were getting ready to move deeper into the forest near the mountains," Sarah said. "We had a farm near there, so we are familiar with the land. It is rugged country, and the forester seldom comes."

"I have a shovel," Simon said. "I can help."

"Gather your things. We will start today," Moshe said.

They packed up their meager belongings, filling the pack with potatoes and beets. Simon carefully tucked in his slingshot.

"Can you use that?" Rutka asked.

Simon nodded and pulled out several rabbit skins he had scraped and dried. "Put them inside your shoes. They will keep your feet warmer."

Rutka's shoes were falling apart and were not much more than a thin covering of leather. She gratefully tucked the fur around her feet.

Simon's shoes were too small. He had grown in spite of the lack of food. Except for holes in the toes, they were still good. He put on his extra pair of socks and nodded to Moshe and Sarah. "We are ready."

Moshe turned without speaking and set off at a steady pace. They walked all day, and by evening they reached a road cutting through the forest.

Moshe squatted down and motioned for them to do the same. "The Germans have bunkers here and there along this road," he whispered. "We must be very careful crossing."

"Our farm is not far," Sarah said. "The Germans took it and we were sent to a ghetto. We went to the forest instead."

"We will wait until dark to cross," Moshe said. "On the other side the land dips down sharply. There is a ravine with a stream. We will follow it until we find a spot."

Simon was cold and hungry, and the pain in his ribs was so severe that he wasn't sure how much longer he could go on. Rutka gave him a worried look. "Are you all right?" she whispered.

"I'll make it," Simon whispered gamely.

Now and then a soldier came out of the bunkers and walked around, giving them the chance to mark where the bunkers were located. As soon as it was dark, Moshe stood up. "We'll go between those two bunkers," he said, pointing to a bunker where they had seen a soldier enter.

With Moshe leading the way, they silently crossed the road. The other side dropped off immediately, and Simon had to grab hold of a small bush to keep from falling. Sarah was not so fortunate. She stumbled over a boulder and, with a scream, tumbled over and over to the bottom of the ravine.

They sat on a rock, rubbing their numb feet, and painfully put their shoes back on. They left the ravine and climbed a hill.

The sun was rising, bright but without warmth. They came to a waterfall, but still Moshe pressed on. Simon's ribs hurt when he breathed deeply, and he knew from Sarah's pinched face that she was in terrible pain. Moshe slowed his pace to accommodate them. He cut Sarah a crutch from a forked branch. Finally, they reached a small meadow. A forest of oak trees mixed with some spruce surrounded the meadow. "Our new home," Moshe declared.

After a few minutes of rest, Moshe set right to work pacing off where they would dig. "We need to be close to the forest but far enough away to dig through roots."

Deciding on a spot, he picked up the shovel. "The ground is frozen," he grunted. He looked up from his work. "You two go and get large branches for the roof."

Rutka and Simon walked into the woods. They found many branches knocked down by windstorms and dragged them back to the site, making trip after trip until Moshe determined they had enough. Then Simon took a turn with the shovel. Luckily, only the first few inches were frozen. After that the digging was easier, although they had to pull out several large rocks. Simon did not last long, and Rutka took over. "I feel so bad I can't help," Sarah fretted. Moshe had wrapped her ankle, which was very swollen and had turned purple.

"I don't think it is broken," Moshe said. "It is a bad sprain, though, and you need to stay off it." He carried her over to the brush pile. "See if you can weave us some kind of door."

Happy to be sharing the work, Sarah chose long twigs and started weaving them into a mat. Rutka pointed to the pile of dirt from the digging. "We had better get rid of that," she said. Using the bucket, they took turns carrying the dirt to the forest and spreading it around. By evening they had a large home dug out under the ground.

"This corner will be the kitchen," Moshe said. He dug a small fire pit and lined it with rocks.

"This corner will be the girls' bedroom, and the boys will sleep here," he said, pointing to another corner. He had dug out a small room at one end. "This will be our bathroom." Rutka gathered handfuls of pine needles and covered the floor several inches deep.

"Good thinking," Moshe said. "That will keep us warmer and dryer."

They arranged a few branches over the hole. "We can finish tomorrow," Moshe said.

Even with the fall, Sarah had not lost her pack. Inside were two small pots. Moshe took one back to the stream for water. Then Sarah made a fire in the pit. With the knife, she cut up an onion and a potato from their small store and boiled them into a warm and satisfying soup.

They each had to drink a few sips from the pan and pass it to the next person. "I will make us some bowls," Moshe promised.

"The potatoes won't last long," Rutka said.

Simon patted his slingshot. "Don't worry. Tomorrow I will get us a rabbit," he said.

Rutka made a snorting sound. "I'll bet I could get one if I could practice a little."

Simon curled up on the fragrant pine needles and closed his eyes. Even though he was still hungry and he was sleeping in a house that looked like a grave, he was happier than he had been since Jozef had been taken. It was almost like having a family again. "I'll teach you tomorrow," he mumbled as he drifted off to sleep.

The next morning they worked on a roof, placing the branches across the opening. Over the main part they stretched the oilcloth, and Moshe dug out a space to store wood for cooking. Later, Rutka and Simon went into the forest. Armed with good-sized rocks, they sat motionless on a fallen log, watching for game. They did not have to wait long before a red squirrel ran down a tree trunk a few feet away. Simon took careful aim, but before he could shoot, the squirrel scampered away.

After another hour, they managed to kill a brown hare. Simon cleaned it, carefully burying the entrails, while Rutka practiced with the slingshot. She had a good eye, and soon she was able to hit her mark nearly every time. They hunted for a few more hours before giving up and heading back to their shelter.

Moshe made a spit out of forked sticks, and, as soon as it was dark, they roasted the meat. Rutka smacked her lips. "This is delicious. I haven't had any meat for a year."

"Tomorrow I am going down to the farms," Moshe said as he doused the fire. Sarah looked alarmed. She had spent most of the day with her foot propped up on the pack. It was still horribly swollen.

"There are people living in our house," Moshe said. "Perhaps they will help us. If not them, perhaps our old neighbors will help. They don't have much themselves, but they are good people."

"Good people are turning in Jews," Simon said.

"Not all. Didn't you find people who helped you?"

Simon nodded, thinking of the people who had helped him. Moshe patted Sarah's shoulder. "Don't worry. I will be all right."

"I will go with you," Simon said.

Moshe shook his head. "You are in no shape for such a long walk." He looked at Rutka, and she nodded in agreement.

"Good, we'll leave in the morning," Moshe said.

chapter thirteen

Freedom

Moshe and Rutka left early. Sarah sat with a small prayer book she always kept near her. Simon went out to empty the bucket and then to fetch water in the pot. In the afternoon, he caught a squirrel and a rabbit. Fearing that the meat would spoil, Sarah cooked them both as soon as it was dark. They ate some and saved the rest for Rutka and Moshe.

The hours dragged by slowly. "Maybe they got lost," Simon said.

Sarah shook her head. "Moshe knows this land. He will not get lost."

Just then they heard rustling outside and Rutka's voice said cheerfully, "We are back."

Lifting Sarah's woven doorway, they pushed in several burlap bags. "It took us a long time because we were carrying all this," Rutka said, hugging Simon. "We had to stop and rest for awhile."

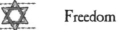

Rutka and Moshe ate the rest of the meat. "It is too dark to see what we have brought back tonight. Let's sleep now and you will see tomorrow."

In the morning the treasures were revealed. "We went to our house first," Moshe told Sarah. "When they opened the door, I could see a crucifix and other religious pictures on the wall. 'I see you are Christians,' I said. 'Your religion tells you to be charitable, does it not?'"

"The man got angry," Rutka said. "'Not to Dirty Jews,' he said. 'Get out before I fetch the Gestapo.'"

"'But this is my house,' I said," Moshe continued the story. "'My father built it with his own hands. Surely you can spare some food.'"

"'Jews cannot own land,' the man told us. 'We petitioned the German government. They gave us this house.'"

Moshe dumped out the contents of the burlap bags. "Fortunately, our old neighbors are a credit to their faith."

Simon gasped. The first bag was full of potatoes and onions. The second bag held even more amazing treats. Inside was a pipe to make a chimney for the fire, two smooth wooden bowls and two spoons, another cooking pot, a second bucket to carry water, a small tin of tea leaves, a bottle of aspirin, a small sack of oats, carrots, apples, and four ripe pears. In addition, there was an extra blanket, and the woman had given Rutka a warm pair of boots.

They ate the pears, savoring every bite. "Even though we have a good supply of food, we will have to make it last," Moshe said. "Who knows when we will get more? Our neighbors are not much better off than we are. The Germans took their cow and much of their crops."

Moshe dug storage places for the food, lining them with pine needles to keep the potatoes dry.

Simon did not have any luck hunting that day, but Sarah made a stew with the carrots and potatoes. She added the bones from the rabbit and squirrel for flavoring. They took turns with the bowls and spoons. Afterward, they shared one cup of tea. Moshe insisted that Sarah and Simon each take one of the aspirin tablets. For the first time in days, Simon could breathe without pain.

The next morning they awoke to snow. Moshe was pleased. "At least while the snow is on the ground we will be hidden," he said. "We have everything we need."

For the next four days they stayed in their shelter. It was dark but surprisingly warm. The bathroom bucket became smelly, so Moshe dug another hole and buried the contents of the bucket. They spent time talking quietly and sleeping.

One morning, they awoke to water dripping through the roof logs. Moshe dug small ditches throughout the room, but by the time the sun had melted all the snow, the floor was muddy, and the pine coverings were soaked.

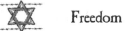

Moshe went for fresh water while Rutka and Simon went hunting. Rutka was usually talkative, but today she was silent and seemed despondent. Simon tried to entertain her with an impersonation of a Nazi officer trying to catch a rabbit. Usually his clowning brought a smile, but today she hardly looked up. Impulsively, Simon put his arm around her shoulders, realizing that he had grown taller than her. "What is it?" he asked gently. Any show of affection usually brought a rude comment from Rutka, but to his surprise, she leaned her head against his shoulder.

"Everyone thought the war would be over in 1942. And then they said surely in 1943. Now it is almost spring of 1944. Is it ever going to end? Other girls are going to school and parties. I am muddy. I haven't had a bath in months. I've got lice and I am ugly."

Simon turned her face to his. "You are brave and you are beautiful. Someday we will be free. Don't give up hope now. Moshe thinks the Russians or the Americans will invade Poland and help free us."

A flicker of hope flashed in Rutka's eyes. She managed a weak grin. "Do you really think I am beautiful?"

When Simon shyly nodded, she laughed. "It must be my wonderful hairstyle that makes you say that." They both laughed. Their hair was matted and greasy, and white nits clung to each hair.

"Remember that little waterfall we saw?" Simon asked. "When it gets warmer we will go there and take a shower."

The winter passed slowly. When it snowed they stayed underground for fear of leaving footprints. Twice more, Moshe returned to the neighbors, returning with enough food to keep them alive. When Simon went with him, he begged the woman for soap, and she gave him a strong-smelling bar and a comb.

As soon as the days were warm enough, Simon and Rutka went to the waterfall. They took turns standing guard while the other one bathed. Their clothes were little more than rags, but they scrubbed them and hung them across some bushes to dry. While they waited, each wrapped in a blanket, they combed each other's hair. When they returned, Moshe and Sarah did the same.

A few weeks later, Rutka and Simon returned to the waterfall, intending to bathe again. Rutka choked back a scream and pointed. A man was hanging from a tree. He had been there for several days, and his face had turned black and his tongue protruded. Black flies buzzed around the body. They stumbled away and ran back to their shelter. When Moshe heard their story, he went to the waterfall. After he returned, his face was grim.

"I met some partisans on the trail, and they told me the man was a collaborator. He was caught with a transmitter sending information to the SS. The partisans had a cabin near here, but since they don't know what information the collaborator sent, they think it is too dangerous to stay in this area. We must move away from here, too."

They quickly packed their meager possessions and started out. Only a few miles away they found a deeply forested spot, choked with brambles and vines. They all took turns digging the new shelter. On top of the log roof they piled brambles, and it was hidden so well that unless a person were right next to it, nobody would ever notice.

Sarah's ankle had healed, although she walked with a slight limp. She scoured the forest for edible plants and mushrooms, and once brought back a handful of sweet wild strawberries. In spite of their efforts, Simon was still always hungry. With so many people hiding in the forest, there was little left to hunt. Sometimes more than a week went by without seeing a rabbit. Simon's body had shot up and he was nearly as tall as Moshe, although he was rail thin, and the constant hunger made him feel weak.

*****

One day, in early October, a group of partisans stepped out of the woods when Simon was hunting. Simon jumped up, ready to run, but the leader waved weakly. "We won't harm you, boy," he said.

Simon noticed that several of the men were wounded. "Are the Germans following you?" Simon asked, suddenly worried.

"I don't think so. They are too busy destroying Warsaw. We joined with the Home Army and tried to take back the city. We held out for nearly two months, but we failed," one of the men said with disgust. "Now the Germans are blowing up every building."

Simon thought of Mrs. Petroski and the people hidden in her cellar. "What about the people?" he asked.

"Many were killed. The rest were expelled from the city. We heard they were sent to concentration camps. We are trying to find the Russians. The Red Army has liberated parts of Poland."

"Did they free Treblinka?" Simon asked.

"The Germans destroyed Treblinka, trying to hide the evidence of their atrocities. The Russians found a few survivors from an uprising hiding in the forest. They told them that most people were killed within hours of arrival. The SS told them it was just a stop to delouse them. They shaved the prisoners' heads and made them undress, saying their clothes would be treated. Then they went into a chamber where they thought they would shower. Instead, they were gassed. The few prisoners who were not killed had to search the bodies for valuables. Then they had to take the bodies to be burned at the crematoria and clean out the chamber for the next trainload. The Germans blew up the chambers, but they forgot one warehouse. It was full of suitcases, clothes, and tens of thousands of pairs of shoes, many of them very small."

Simon sank to the ground, overcome with grief.

The partisan patted his shoulder. "You knew people who were sent there?"

"My whole family," Simon said numbly.

When the partisans had moved on, Simon walked slowly back to tell the others of the news. Sarah and Rutka cried when he repeated the story. "What should we do?" Sarah asked.

"What can we do? If the partisans are right, the Red Army may be here soon. We will stay here and wait for our liberators," Moshe said.

They talked no more of Treblinka. That night they tried only to think of the future. "The first thing I am going to do when we are free is find someplace to take a bath," Rutka said. "A real bath. I will sit in it until my skin wrinkles."

Sarah nodded. "That does sound wonderful. I used to have some scented bath oil," she added dreamily. "Can you imagine such luxury?"

"I want a bath, too," Simon said. "But then I want to eat until I am stuffed."

"What about you, Moshe?" Rutka asked. "What is the first thing you will do?"

"I will go back to my house and tell those people to get out." He smiled at Sarah. "Then you can take a bath in your own tub. My house is very modern," he bragged. "It has inside water and a water heater. Real warm water anytime you want."

Simon thought of the ones he had lost. His father and mother, Jozef, little Anya. Why did they deserve to die while he lived? If any of them had survived, how would he ever find them? The partisans had told him of other horrors: Jews herded into synagogues and barns and the buildings set on fire, burning them alive. In a town in Russia called Kiev, thirty-three thousand people had been forced to strip off their clothes and pile them into neat piles of shirts, pants, and even underwear, before they were led to a pit and shot, whole families at a time. Yet the men who had done these things would go home when the war was over and live their lives with their own families, as though they had done nothing. He did not share his dark thought out loud, but Rutka took his hand as if she understood what he was thinking.

Surprisingly, Moshe seemed to know what he was thinking, too. One day, when Moshe and Simon were getting water and sticks for the cooking fire, Moshe turned abruptly and said, "You must find a way to put it past you. If you live bitter and apart from people, they have won again. The only real revenge is to have a good life. You can go to America. Didn't you say you have grandparents in America?"

Simon nodded. "I don't want to leave Rutka."

"Maybe your grandparents can help her, too."

*****

The days dragged by slowly and turned into weeks. October passed, and then November and December. January began and still nothing had happened.

Moshe and Simon made several trips back to the road. They found a place where they could observe the German bunkers without being seen. But each time the Nazis were still there, entrenched safely in their bunkers.

Then, at last, one morning they awoke to what sounded like distant thunder. "Artillery!" Moshe said.

Sarah's eyes were wide with fright.

"I will go down and see if I can find out what is happening," Moshe said, with a comforting pat on her shoulder.

Sarah shook her head. "We will all go together," she said firmly.

Moshe and Sarah argued a bit, but Rutka and Simon agreed with Sarah. Moshe reluctantly gave in. They made their way so they could see what was happening. The Germans were running. Abandoning the bunkers, they piled into trucks and fled. Simon and the others watched

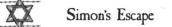

intently for an hour before the Russian army came into sight with tanks, trucks, and a large group of bedraggled and defeated German prisoners marching before them.

With Moshe in the lead, they walked down to the road, where they were immediately surrounded by Russian soldiers brandishing their weapons. The soldiers did not speak Polish. Their leader looked at them suspiciously and it was obvious he wanted to shoot them.

"Maybe they think we are spies," Sarah cried in Yiddish.

The soldier in charge of the group stared at Sarah. "Jew?" he asked.

When they nodded he went to a high-ranking officer and spoke briefly. The officer returned with him and asked in Yiddish, "You are all Jews?"

Moshe nodded. "We have been hiding in the forest for more than two years."

The officer still looked suspicious. "How is that possible?"

Moshe told them of the underground shelter and the fight to stay alive. "Show me," the officer demanded.

They led him back to the camp. The officer shook his head in amazement. "Do you have a place to go?"

"He had a farm, but the Nazis gave it to a Polish family," Simon stammered the words out angrily in Yiddish.

The officer stared thoughtfully at Simon. "How far away is your home?"

Moshe shrugged. "Five kilometers by the road, three or four through the forest."

"Follow me." The officer stepped at a brisk pace back to the road, where his soldiers were busy stripping supplies from the bunkers and loading them onto a large truck.

"What do you think he is going to do?" Rutka asked.

"I don't know," Simon answered.

Without turning around the officer said, "We are going to get this man's farm back." He snapped out some orders, and a minute later two jeeps with drivers and guards pulled up beside them.

"Can it be true?" Sarah whispered "Is it really over?"

A minute later, they were bouncing down the road toward Moshe's former home. Rutka sat beside Simon. He took her hand and squeezed it.

"I am afraid," Rutka said slowly. "What kind of world will it be now? What if there are no Jewish people left but us?"

They pulled up in front of a small stone house and the officer jumped out of the jeep. With his crop handle, he rapped on the door. A man's and a woman's frightened faces peered out. Behind them Simon saw several children.

"You are to vacate this house," the officer said in perfect Polish. "You may have fifteen minutes."

"It is my house," the man said boldly. "The Gestapo gave me a paper." He disappeared inside the house and returned a minute later with an official document.

The officer studied the paper the man handed him. Then he calmly tore it to pieces. "The Germans are no longer in charge. If I were you, I would worry that this paper might make me considered a collaborator."

The woman and children were crying. Sarah touched the officer's sleeve. "Where can they go?" she asked with a stricken look on her face.

Before the officer could answer, Moshe said, "Did they worry about us when I came for help?"

"There are children," Sarah said softly.

"And where are our children? A whole generation of Jewish children."

"The Red Cross is setting up shelters," the officer said. "They can go there. Or maybe their Polish friends will treat them with Christian kindness," he added with a sharp laugh.

They watched silently while the family trudged away down the road, carrying their possessions.

Sarah leaned her head against Moshe's shoulder. The officer smiled for the first time. "You have your house back." With that he climbed back into his jeep, gave a jaunty salute, and roared away.

The others followed quickly, sitting and sliding most of the way, but Sarah's scream had been heard. Simon heard shouts in German above him. Suddenly, the sky was lit up with a flare, and gunshots kicked up the dirt around them. Moshe had reached Sarah and was urging her to her feet. "Run," he yelled as another flare went off.

The ravine was clogged with thick bushes and vines. Holding his side, Simon ran blindly. The bushes scratched and pulled on his clothes, but he kept running. He could hear Rutka nearby, and behind them Moshe came, half carrying Sarah. After a minute, the shooting stopped.

Moshe caught up to them with Sarah. "I am so sorry," she cried. "I almost got us caught."

"We may be yet. I think they have given up for now, but we will have to go farther than I planned. I am afraid they will look in the morning. They may bring dogs."

"Dogs can't get a scent in the water," Rutka said. "I hear a stream." Guided by their ears, for it was much too dark to see, they reached the stream. "The water will be freezing," Sarah said. "Take off your shoes. At least we will have something warm to put on."

The stream was so icy it felt like pinpricks on their skin. Moshe climbed out and circled back, hoping to confuse any dogs. Sarah leaned against Moshe, and Simon took her other side so that they could almost carry her between them. At last, Moshe was satisfied that they would not be tracked.

Moshe moved first. He headed for the house.

"What are you doing?" Sarah asked.

"I am making a bath," Moshe said. "When we are clean and fed, we will go to the Red Cross and see if Simon's grandparents are looking for him. Simon can search for some word about his family, and Rutka can see about her aunt and uncle. In the meantime, you children can stay with us."

Simon looked at Rutka, who suddenly looked alarmed at the mention of Simon's grandparents. "Don't worry. I am not going anywhere without you. We'll search for our families and then begin a new journey."

"Your grandparents may not like that idea very much," Rutka said.

"I have been thinking a lot about Palestine," Simon said seriously. "They will need people to build a great country. A place where Jewish people can live proudly and be free."

"Then we will go to Palestine," Rutka said. "After what we have been through, I think we can do anything."

 the end

The Real History Behind the Story

Simon is a fictional character, but many of his experiences belong to actual Holocaust survivors. Although no one knows exactly how many Jewish people the Nazis murdered, estimates of 6 million are generally accepted. About 3.5 million Jewish people—about 10 percent of the population—lived in Poland at the start of World War II. Although there were periodic outbreaks of violence in the nineteenth and twentieth centuries, for the most part the Jews in Poland prospered. Many people fled into Russia when Adolf Hitler came to power in Germany. Many stayed, however—perhaps like Mr. Gorski in the story, thinking that there would be safety in numbers.

The Warsaw Ghetto

The Germans attacked Warsaw, the largest city in Poland, with air raids and bombs on September 1, 1939. The Polish army only managed to hold out until September 27, 1939.

The German authorities set up a Jewish council and a civic leader, Adam Czerniaków, was picked to lead it. The purpose of the council was to make sure German orders were carried out. Czerniaków committed suicide when the deportations started rather than obey a Nazi order to deport six thousand people a day to Treblinka.

154

This map shows the major ghettos in German-occupied Europe during World War II, including Warsaw, the largest ghetto established by the Nazis.

Three destitute young children sit on the pavement in the Warsaw ghetto. Conditions in the ghetto were deplorable.

The orders came quickly. Every male from age sixteen to sixty had to report for work. Everyone older than ten had to wear a blue Star of David on a white armband. Jewish people could not own property. They were only allowed to ride marked streetcars, bank accounts were frozen, and strict curfews were imposed. These restrictions were difficult enough, but in October 1940, the Nazis announced the formation of a "Jewish Quarter" in a two-mile-wide area in the center section of the city. All Jews were required to move there. The 350,000 Jews in Warsaw and Jews from the nearby towns were also ordered there, swelling the population to 400,000. Many people arrived at the ghetto with little more than the clothes on their backs. The Germans issued rations of about eight hundred calories per day—not enough to ward off starvation. Later, even this was cut.

The authorities required the Jews to build a wall around the ghetto. It was ten feet high with barbed wire on top. Nevertheless, smugglers moved in and out of the ghetto, bringing in needed food. The punishment for being caught smuggling was death.

Deportations

The Germans tightened their grip on the ghetto residents. All libraries and schools were closed. Radios were forbidden. Because so many people were crowded into such a small area, disease took a heavy toll. Some months there were as many as five thousand deaths from starvation and disease.

When the deportations began in July 1942, some people volunteered to go, believing that they were to be trained as farm workers. Soon, rumors began to circulate that the people were being killed and the Germans were rounding up victims. At first, they took them off the streets, and later, to make quotas of five to six thousand a day, they began to systematically empty the buildings in the ghetto.

Treblinka, a Nazi death camp, was built about fifty miles from Warsaw as part of the "final solution"—the Nazi-coordinated plan to murder all the Jews of Europe. At first a labor camp, a second part was opened in 1942 when the deportations started. It had a gas chamber disguised as a bathhouse. Victims were packed in so tightly that they died

A large group of Jews forced into cattle cars during a deportation from the Warsaw ghetto to the death camp, Treblinka. Many thousands of Jews were deported from Warsaw to Treblinka, where virtually all of them perished.

standing up. At first, the bodies were buried. But later, crematoria were built to burn the remains. Many people died within two hours of reaching the camp.

Resistance in Warsaw

Heinrich Himmler ordered the destruction of the Warsaw ghetto on April 19, 1943. German forces began to destroy the ghetto. The Jewish Fighting Organization (ZOB) fought them for over a month before the ghetto was destroyed. Mordecai Anielewicz, the leader, was killed or took his own life along with many companions in a bunker on May 8.

The Polish resistance tried to take back Warsaw a year later on August 1, 1944, and were also defeated. The Germans then destroyed most of the city.

Although many Polish people betrayed their Jewish friends and neighbors, many others hid and protected Jews. The punishment for helping a Jew was death, not only for that person but also the whole family. Still, after the war Jewish people stepped out of attics, basements, and barns where they had been hiding for years. One social worker named Irena Sendler and her helpers even managed to smuggle 2,500 babies out of the Warsaw ghetto.

End of the Holocaust

Hitler committed suicide in April 1945. The Germans surrendered on May 8, 1945. As American, British, and Soviet troops liberated the camps in Poland and Germany, the full horror of the Nazis' inhumanity was revealed. The few survivors were so thin and weak they resembled skeletons. Many died of starvation and disease even after being liberated. Displaced persons (DP) camps were set up for the survivors, and slowly they began to emigrate to such places as America and Palestine. Even after the war, the British, who controlled Palestine, tried to block immigration. In 1948, the British withdrew, and the nation of Israel was established.

Further Reading

Fiction

Glatshteyn, Yankev. *Emil and Karl.* New Milford, Conn.: Roaring Book Press, 2006.

Orlev, Uri. *Run, Boy, Run.* Boston: Houghton Mifflin, 2001.

Spring, Debbie. *The Righteous Smuggler.* Toronto: Second Story Press, 2005.

Nonfiction

Boraks-Nemetz, Lilian and Irene N. Watts, eds. *Tapestry of Hope: Holocaust Writing for Young People.* Plattsburg, N.Y.: Tundra Books of Northern New York, 2003.

Roy, Jennifer. *Yellow Star.* New York: Marshall Cavendish, 2006.

Zullo, Allan, and Mara Bovsun. *Survivors: True Stories of Children in the Holocaust.* New York: Scholastic, 2004.

Internet Addresses

United States Holocaust Memorial Museum
<http://www.ushmm.org/>

USC Shoah Foundation Institute
<http://college.usc.edu/vhi/>

Yad Vashem: The Holocaust Martyrs' and Heroes' Remembrance Authority
<http://www.yadvashem.org/>